SPIDER
WOMAN
STORIES

Legends of the Hopi Indians

SPIDER WOMAN STORIES

Selected and Interpreted by

G. M. MULLETT

The University of Arizona Press
Tucson, Arizona

GEORGE CRAWFORD MERRICK MULLETT was for several years a regular contributor of stories to *St. Nicholas* magazine and other periodicals for children. Her lifelong interest in American Indians dated from her childhood in the Serpent Mound area of Ohio. It was enhanced by her association with Jesse Walter Fewkes with whom she worked as a scientific illustrator for the Bureau of Ethnology, the Smithsonian Institution, from 1910 to 1928. His *Designs on Prehistoric Pottery from the Mimbres Valley, N.M.* and many other works contain illustrations by Mrs. Mullett.

Seventh printing 1991

THE UNIVERSITY OF ARIZONA PRESS

Text Copyright© 1979, Arizona Board of Regents
Illustrations Copyright© 1979,
by Suzanne M. Smith
All Rights Reserved
Manufactured in the U.S.A.

Library of Congress Cataloging in Publication Data

Mullett, G. M.
    Spider Woman stories.

    SUMMARY: Presents Hopi Indian legends of the Creation, the adventures of the hero Tiyo, and the Twin War Gods and their activities on behalf of the Hopi.
    1. Hopi Indians—Legends. 2. Indians of North America—Arizona—Legends. [1. Hopi Indians—Legends. 2. Indians of North America—Legends] I. Title.
E99.H7M86 398.2'09791 78-11556
ISBN 0-8165-0669-8
ISBN 0-8165-0621-3 pbk.

No men of the stone age have a richer traditional mythology than the Hopi Indians. The unrecorded literature of this people contains no more beautiful expression of their aboriginal thought than the story of the adventures of Tiyo (the Youth), one of their culture heroes on his visit to the Underworld. The nobility of thought expressed in this epic reveals a people far advanced in poetic development, their legends needing only the proper setting to interest the literary world. There is in this legend something higher than an Indian tale, for there pervades in it the yearning common to all people, the desire for an intimate knowledge of the meaning of life, especially the future of the human soul and its life after death of the body.

JESSE WALTER FEWKES

Contents

Foreword, by Fred Eggan   ix

Preface   xv

First Tale   1

The Story of Tiyo   7

    Tiyo Meets Spider Woman   15

    Tiyo Travels Through the Underworld   21

    Tiyo Appears Before Snake Mana   29

    Tiyo Returns Home   33

    Tiyo Rejoins His Clan   37

The Youth Who Brought the Corn   44

The Twins Visit Tawa   54

Puukonhoya Wins a Bride   62

The Youth Conquers Man-Eagle   78

The Youth and the Eagles   90

The Children and the Hummingbird   108

The Antelope Maid   118

The Giant Elk   127

The Coyote and the Water Serpent   132

Further Reading   141

Foreword

SPIDER WOMAN STORIES provides readers with a unique glimpse into the mythological world of the Hopi Indians of northern Arizona, who have resided in their pueblos on Black Mesa for at least a thousand years. These stories, and many others, have been handed down from generation to generation by word of mouth; not until the late nineteenth century did anthropologists begin to write them down. Scholars first attempted to utilize Hopi myths and legends to reconstruct Hopi history, but Mrs. George M. Mullett has seen them as literature and has presented them in a "poetic prose" that engages our attention and interest.

Mrs. Mullett first became acquainted with the Hopi Indians through her association with Jesse Walter Fewkes, a former director of the Bureau of American Ethnology, Smithsonian Institution, who began a study of the Hopis in the late 1880s and continued it for many years. The Snake Dance immediately attracted his attention because he had been trained as a zoologist, and he set about to study it with the aid of A.M.

Stephen, who had been living at Keams Canyon for a decade and was becoming fluent in both Navajo and Hopi. Together with J. G. Owens, they published the first detailed scientific account of "The Snake Ceremonials at Walpi" (*A Journal Of American Ethnology and Archaeology*, vol. 4, 1894), which included "The Legend of Tí-yo, the Snake Hero" as recorded by Stephen from the chief priest of the Antelope Society. This legend provides an explanation of the origins of the Snake clan and ceremony, and its relations to the Antelope Society with which it is associated. It is also one of the most dramatic accounts in the whole Hopi repertoire.

The Hopi Indians believe that they emerged from the Underworld through the *sipapu*, or opening, which is located in the bottom of the Grand Canyon, from whence different groups traveled around and had various adventures before arriving at their present locations. Recent research indicates that the early Hopi homeland was in the western Mojave desert and that ancestral groups gradually moved eastward, some residing in the lower reaches of the Grand Canyon during the tenth to twelfth centuries, before joining their relatives in their present locations on the southern spurs of Black Mesa.

Hopi cosmology provides no clear-cut creation legend so Mrs. Mullett, in her First Tale, provides a turn-of-the-century version in which Tawa, the Sun God, and Spider Woman, the Earth Goddess, willed the various aspects of the world into being. In my experience this version is closer to the Zuni conception of creation than to the Hopi and provides Spider Woman with a more important role than most Hopi will admit today. The Story of Tiyo is next presented in six sections, following generally the Stephen version obtained in 1893. Here Mrs. Mullett has employed her knowledge of Hopi life gained from a long period of professional association as an artist and illustrator to interpret the events of Tiyo's journey to make the story more comprehensible to lay readers. The other legends are primarily concerned with the Twin War Gods and their activities on behalf of the Hopi. These twins are children of the Sun and Water, but Spider Woman as their "grandmother" plays an important role in their accomplishments. Their visit to their father, the Sun, where they are tested in various ways, and their adventures with various giant animals and monsters, will strike familiar chords, and may entice some readers to explore the original versions such as are now available in Stephen's "Hopi Tales" (*Journal Of American Folklore*, vol. 42, 1929) and other sources.

The story of Tiyo involves the youth's journey down the Colorado River in a hollow log to the land of the snakes, at a time when animals and human beings were much closer to one another and animals could assume human forms. When the rapids ceased and the youth was able to land he met Spider Woman, who invited him into her house. Here she represents the trap-door spider who lives underground in a "kiva," which in itself is the symbol of the Underworld from which mankind emerged. And long ago she taught the Hopi how to spin and weave cotton.

Under the guidance of Spider Woman the youth entered the land of the snakes and learned the secrets of the Snake-Antelope kiva, where he ultimately won the Snake maiden as his bride-to-be. Continuing on to the kiva of the Woman of Hard Substances, located in the western ocean, the youth met the sun on its daily journey across the skies and back under the world, and was taken on a tour of the various deities who promote the growth and fecundity of plants and animals, as well as human beings, before being allowed to return to his home village near Navajo Mountain with his Snake-maiden bride.

From their union were produced both snakes and the human members of the Snake clan, and the rituals which the youth had learned formed the basis for the ceremonies of the Antelope and Snake societies, in which the snakes who are caught in the four directions are made "brothers" in the Snake Society before being carried back to the desert to take the Hopi prayers for rain to the deities of the directions. But initially the snakes produced by the union of the youth and his Snake bride bit the village children and led to removal of the population to other locations. Tiyo and his bride were readmitted only when he had won a place for them by besting Masauwuh, the deity who controlled the surface of the earth and was in charge of death.

Originally the Snake Dance was performed in all the major villages of the Hopi, alternating annually with the Flute Ceremony. In the late 1970s it no longer was performed at Walpi, but could still be seen at Shongopavi and Mishongnovi on Second Mesa and at Hotevila on Third Mesa. The public performance, which attracts a tremendous crowd of Indians and whites, is perhaps the most dramatic ritual which has survived in native North America. Preceding the dance in the plaza, the priests of the Antelope and Snake societies carry out rituals which dramatize the adventures of Tiyo and the Snake maiden and symbolize the bravery of the members of the Snake society, who once were the warriors who helped protect the villages against enemy attacks. As the dancers take the snakes into their mouths and circle the plaza the audience sits in deep silence. More often than not the prayers for rain carried to the four directions by the snakes are soon answered by showers — while the members of the Snake Society purify themselves and remain in seclusion in the kiva for the requisite four days.

These brief remarks suggest another dimension to the Spider Woman stories that Mrs. Mullett presents to us. She early saw their interest and with the help of Dr. Fewkes she has presented them in a form which makes them intelligible to a wider audience. Today the Hopi are more aware of their cultural heritage and are themselves actively engaged in recording their songs and ceremonies, and we can look forward to new interpretations. In the meantime we can thank Suzanne M. Smith, Mrs. Mullett's daughter, for rescuing these stories from obscurity and making them available to a new generation of readers.

FRED EGGAN
Professor Emeritus
Department of Anthropology
The University of Chicago

Preface

George M. Mullett wrote *Spider Woman Stories* as would a news reporter after many interviews and talks with a world authority on Hopi Indians, Jesse Walter Fewkes of the Bureau of Ethnology, Smithsonian Institution, Washington, D.C. Mrs. Mullett likened the Hopi tales to Greek myths, which she knew better than the history of her own family. Besides being a scientific illustrator for the Bureau of Ethnology, she also was a writer published in magazines such as the *St. Nicholas*. When Mrs. Mullett expressed an interest in the Hopi stories related to her by Dr. Fewkes, he encouraged her to write a more readable version than had thus far been published, and one which would be as faithful to the primary source material. This she did, to his satisfaction and delight. He also requested illustrations, some of which are used on the back of this book, which she completed sometime between 1917 and 1919.

Other versions (including some by Fewkes) of many of the Hopi tales had already been published. These were, however, primarily straightforward records of interviews with Hopi tribal members and firsthand observations of Hopi ceremonials. An example is the 1894 version of the Snake ceremonials at Walpi obtained by A.M. Stephen directly from the Hopis. A reference list to aid the reader interested in these earlier versions is located in the section of this book entitled "Further Reading."

Fewkes was second leader of the Hemenway Southwestern Archaeological Expedition, commissioned by Mary Hemenway, a Boston philanthropist, in 1889. In 1891 the expedition focused on the Moqui or Hopi villages of Arizona, and A. M. Stephen became Fewkes's assistant until the deaths of Stephen and Mrs. Hemenway in 1894. Fewkes was editor, commentator, and analyst from a scientific viewpoint and Stephen, transcriber. As early as 1884 and 1885 Stephen had recorded three versions of the Tiyo story. Stephen's last version was published in Fewkes's "The Snake Ceremonials at Walpi" in the *Journal of American Ethnology and Archaeology,* vol. 4, 1894. Elsie C. Parsons, editor of the two-volume *Hopi Journal of Alexander M. Stephen,* 1936, characterized the earlier Stephen writings as "more Navajo than Hopi," having been recorded by Stephen when he knew only Navajo. Other Hopi tales by both Fewkes and Stephen were published in the *Journal of American Folklore* prior to the Mullett writings. Even so, as Dr. Fewkes saw it, the Tiyo Hopi legend needed only poetic handling to make it an epic.

When my mother gave me the manuscript in 1940, she asked me to "find a publisher." I am grateful that Sam Stanley, Research Anthropologist and Coordinator for the Program of the Center for the Study of Man, the Smithsonian Institution, read the manuscript and encouraged me to find a publisher.

I also wish to thank Fred Eggan, who, besides writing the Foreword for the book, inspired and encouraged me to research Hopi myths that had been published before 1918. A result of that research is the Further Reading section of this book. Two people in the Smithsonian Institution also assisted me: my thanks go to Jack Marquardt, Research Librarian of the Museum of Natural History, and to Janette K. Saquet, Anthropology Branch Librarian.

I would like to say a special thanks to my family, who gave me the impetus to pursue this project to its completion. My husband Gordon, my daughter Daisy, and son Victor helped with proofreading and good advice. Gratitude is also due the University of Arizona Press for effecting publication, and particularly to Pat Shelton and Marshall Townsend.

SUZANNE MULLETT SMITH

First Tale

IN THE BEGINNING there were only two: Tawa, the Sun God, and Spider Woman, the Earth Goddess. All the mysteries and power in the Above belonged to Tawa, while Spider Woman controlled the magic of the Below. In the Underworld, abode of the gods, they dwelt and they were All. There was neither man nor woman, bird nor beast, no living thing until these Two willed it to be.

In time it came to them that there should be other gods to share their labors. So Tawa divided himself and there came Muiyinwuh, God of All Life Germs; Spider Woman also divided herself so that there was Huzruiwuhti, Woman of the Hard Substances, the goddess of all hard ornaments of wealth such as coral, turquoise, silver and shell. Huzruiwuhti became the always-bride of Tawa. They were the First Lovers and of their union there came into being those marvelous ones the Magic Twins—Puukonhoya, the Youth, and Palunhoya, the Echo. As time unrolled there followed Hicanavaiya, Ancient of Six (the Four World Quarters, the Above and

Below), Man-Eagle, the Great Plumed Serpent and many others. But Masauwuh, the Death God, did not come of these Two but was bad magic who appeared only after the making of creatures.

And then it came about that these Two had one Thought and it was a mighty Thought — that they would make the Earth to be between the Above and the Below where now lay shimmering only the Endless Waters. So they sat them side by side, swaying their beautiful bronze bodies to the pulsing music of their own great voices, making the First Magic Song, a song of rushing winds and flowing waters, a song of light and sound and life.

"I am Tawa," sang the Sun God, "I am Light. I am Life. I am Father of all that shall ever come."

"I am Kokyanwuhti," the Spider Woman crooned in softer note. "I receive Light and nourish Life. I am Mother of all that shall ever come."

"Many strange thoughts are forming in my mind—beautiful forms of birds to float in the Above, of beasts to move upon the Earth and fish to swim in the Waters," intoned Tawa.

"Now let these things that move in the Thought of my lord appear," chanted Spider Woman, the while with her slender fingers she caught up clay from beside her and made the Thoughts of Tawa take form. One by one she shaped them and laid them aside—but they breathed not nor moved.

"We must do something about this," said

Tawa. "It is not good that they lie thus still and quiet. Each thing that has a form must also have a spirit. So now, my beloved, we must make a mighty Magic."

They laid a white blanket over the many figures, a cunningly woven woolen blanket, fleecy as a cloud, and made a mighty incantation over it, and soon the figures stirred and breathed.

"Now, let us make ones like unto you and me, so that they may rule over and enjoy these lesser creatures," sang Tawa, and Spider Woman shaped the Thoughts of her lord into man figures and woman figures like unto their own. But after the blanket magic had been made the figures still stayed inert. So Spider Woman gathered them all in her arms and cradled them in her warm young bosom, while Tawa bent his glowing eyes upon them. The two now sang the magic Song of Life over them, and at last each man figure and woman figure breathed and lived.

"Now that was a good thing and a mighty thing," quoth Tawa. "So now all this is finished, and there shall be no new things made by us. Those things we have made shall multiply, each one after his own kind. I will make a journey across the Above each day to shed my light upon them and return each night to Huzruiwuhti. And now I shall go to turn my blazing shield upon the Endless Waters, so that the Dry Land may appear. And this day will be the first day upon the Earth."

"Now I shall lead all these created things

[3]

to the land that you shall cause to appear above the waters," said Spider Woman.

Then Tawa took down his burnished shield from the turquoise wall of the kiva and swiftly mounted his glorious way to the Above. After Spider Woman had bent her wise, all-seeing eyes upon the thronging creatures about her, she wound her way among them, separating them into groups.

"Thus and thus shall you be and thus shall you remain, each one in his own tribe forever. You are Zunis, you are Kohoninos, you are Pah-Utes—." The Hopis, all, all people were named by Kokyanwuhti then.

Placing her Magic Twins beside her, Spider Woman called all the people to follow where she led. Through all the Four Great Caverns of the Underworld she led them, until they finally came to an opening, a sipapu, which led above. This came out at the lowest depth of the Pisisbaiya (the Colorado River) and was the place where the people were to come to gather salt. So lately had the Endless Waters gone down that the Turkey, Koyona, pushing eagerly ahead, dragged his tail feathers in the black mud where the dark bands were to remain forever.

Mourning Dove flew overhead, calling to some to follow, and those who followed where his sharp eyes had spied out springs and built beside them were called "Huwinyamu" after him. So Spider Woman chose a creature to lead each clan to a place to build their house. The Puma, the Snake, the Antelope, the Deer, and other Horn creatures, each led a clan to a place to build their house. Each clan henceforth bore the name of the creature who had led them.

Then Spider Woman spoke to them thus: "The woman of the clan shall build the house, and the family name shall descend through her. She shall be house builder and homemaker. She shall mold the jars for the storing of food and water. She shall grind the grain for food and tenderly rear the young. The man of the clan shall build kivas of stone under the ground where he shall pay homage to his gods. In these kivas the man shall make sand pictures which will be his altars. Of colored sand shall he make them and they shall be called 'ponya'. After council I shall whisper to him; he shall make prayer sticks or paho to place upon the ponya to bear his prayers. There shall be the Wupo Paho, the Great Paho, which is mine. There shall be four paho of blue, the Cawka Paho — one for the great Tawa, one for Muiyinwuh, one for Woman of the Hard Substances and one for the Ancient of Six. Each of these paho must be cunningly and secretly wrought with prayer and song. The man, too, shall weave the clan blankets with their proper symbols. The Snake clan shall have its symbol and the Antelope clan its symbol; thus it shall be for each clan. Man shall fashion himself weapons and furnish his family with game."

Stooping down, she gathered some sand in her hand, letting it run out in a thin, continuous stream. "See the movement of the sand. That is

[5]

the life that will cause all things therein to grow. The Great Plumed Serpent, Lightning, will rear and strike the earth to fertilize it, Rain Cloud will pour down waters and Tawa will smile upon it so that green things will spring up to feed my children."

Her eyes now sought the Above where Tawa was descending toward his western kiva in all the glory of red and gold. "I go now, but have no fear, for we Two will be watching over you. Look upon me now, my children, ere I leave. Obey the words I have given you and all will be well, and if you are in need of help call upon me and I will send my sons to your aid."

The people gazed wide-eyed upon her shining beauty. Her woven upper garment of soft white wool hung tunic-wise over a blue skirt. On its left side was woven a band bearing the woman's symbols, the Butterfly and the Squash Blossom, in designs of red and yellow and green with bands of black appearing between. Her beautiful neck was hung with heavy necklaces of turquoise, shell and coral, and pendants of the same hung from her ears. Her face was fair, with warm eyes and tender red lips, and her form most graceful. Upon her small feet were skin boots of gleaming white, and they now turned toward where the sand spun about in whirlpool fashion. She held up her right hand and smiled upon them, then stepped upon the whirling sand. Wonder of wonders, before their eyes the sands seemed to suck her swiftly down until she disappeared entirely from their sight.

The Story of Tiyo

BACK, FAR BACK, in the mists of time when the world was very young, at Tokonabi lived the Hopi lad Tiyo, of the Puma clan. First-born of his father, the Kikmonwi or village chieftain, he entered the world big with awe for the wonders of creation and a vast thirst for knowledge of their meanings. The eyes of his parents would meet in startled pride to see their wee lad watching the moving stream of sand sifting through the side of his small copper-colored fist and trying to see for himself that Life which his father had told him lay in the earth and caused the corn to sprout; or again, they would find him, ear close to some vessel of his mother's modelling, tapping on it to hear the Spirit of the Bowl make answer.

He would leave his romping to watch her make her brilliant pigments in small earthen vessels of her own molding and very early learned to select and chew a yucca stick into a proper paintbrush. When, with skillful fingers, she wove or painted design upon basket or bowl, there was he to watch her and his quick eyes were ever spying out a new "Why?"

"Why do you leave the black bands around

[7]

the border unfinished, my mother? Why is a gap left?"

"So you saw that did you, little man? Surely you have the sharp eyes of Mourning Dove. Know then and remember that there is the Gate of Life for the Spirit of the Bowl to enter and to leave."

"But sometimes there is no opening," Tiyo would persist.

"Yes, and when it is that way it comes about that it is a burial bowl, so fashioned to hold good food for one who has left to join the Ancestors. A hole must then be knocked in its center so that its Spirit be released to go with the departed one's Breath Body to the Underworld."

The wisdom imparted by his parents passed like trickling water through the ears of his brother and two sisters, but Tiyo was ever held spellbound by the lore of his ancestors and stored and pondered it in his heart. When winter came and the hard, frozen ground held fast prisoner all the evil spirits who might work that one ill who was trying to pry into magic lore, how eagerly did he hang upon the tales whispered by the bolder of the old men. Sitting around glowing pinyon fires to carve the sacred dolls or gaily colored kachina masks, the old men told thrilling tales of those marvellous beings who peopled the Underworld. And when, filled with a tremendous yearning to know more of these mysteries, he would run to his mother with his scraps of knowledge, her eyes would light proudly even while she bantered with him.

[8]

"This is man knowledge—how should I know?" she would answer. "Have thou a care, little wise man, lest you be served the same dumpling as Brother Coyote."

"Tell me, my mother," Tiyo would demand, tugging at her arm and quick to scent a story.

"You know how it comes about that Brother Coyote is always prying into everything? My, but he is a meddlesome one, that one! On a day he was walking across the mesa looking here and there for some mischief when he came upon Tumblebug with his head close to the ground. At first Brother Coyote thought Tumblebug was playing dead, as he so often does, but finally he felt that he must find out. He touched Tumblebug gently with his paw. 'Brother Bug, what are you doing with your ear thus close to the ground?'

"'Yes,' answered the Bug slowly. 'I am listening to the gods talking down there in the Below.'

"'Ah,' returned the Coyote, 'and pray, Brother Tumblebug, what do the gods say?'

"'They say,' said the Bug, glad to have a chance to teach meddlesome Coyote a lesson, 'they say very solemnly that Brother Coyote would do well to run along home and attend to his own business.'"

And then when he had joined in lustily at her laughter at his own expense he would beg for other stories or songs about Brother Coyote, who, being such a busybody and altogether loose character, was always having thrilling adventures.

Now, because Tiyo was first born and because their thoughts were knit so closely together, the Kikmonwi bared his heart to his son. All his fears for his people, because of the thin clouds, small springs and scant rains, were shared with the youth, and his hope to make a great tribe of this small number became Tiyo's also. So when the boy became a youth, well-muscled, clean-limbed and straight, he withdrew himself more and more from the games of his comrades, in which he easily surpassed them all, and gave himself more and more to the counsels of his father or to thoughtful brooding on the cliff's sheer edge.

Seated on the canyon's rim, like an atom hung in the immensity between the Above and Below, he would gaze for hours upon the wonders spread before him. His eager eyes tried to plunge beneath the surface of things that appeared, and the Eagle, Kwahu, himself, mounted no higher than did the questing thought of Tiyo as it strained to fly forth and learn the Why, the Where and the End of All. As he sat there, he watched Tawa march his shining course across the sky's blue arch; he gazed with rapture as the Sun God changed the canyon's walls from orange to pink, from pink to red; marvelled at the magic of him as he caused huge buttes to fade away and vanish and then, pulling long shadows behind him, splash the rocky walls with mighty pictures in a gorgeous riot of color.

Or, on other days when lowering clouds hid Tawa from view, he watched the Great Plumed Serpent, Palulkon, strike and bite the earth, the while his blood would race and thrill as he listened to its angry bellowings thundering and reverberating through gorge and chasm.

But more potently than any of these wonders did the Far-Far-Below River draw his seeking eyes, coming as it seemed from the Unknown and travelling into the Unknown again. Like a great silver serpent it writhed its way, pulling behind it all the waters of his earth and vanishing with them into the Underworld. With such a wealth of water streaming into the Underworld, why could not Tawa on his nightly journey through the same region bring back enough for a bountiful rain for his people who so sorely needed it? But, alas! the rains that now came were so scant that the corn parched and Masauwuh, the Death God, continually skulked about their borders.

At last Tiyo, flaming with a high resolve, made up his mind to follow the Far-Far-Below River, brave every terror of the Underworld, fathom its mysteries, and win from the gods themselves the right to live and flourish.

Eagerly he sought his father: "Inaa, my father," he said, "I have been wondering where the Far-Far-Below River travels."

"So that is what you have been thinking about," said his father. "We do not know very much about that thing."

"I am convinced, after much long thinking,

[11]

Inaa, that the Far-Far-Below River, which daily draws all the waters of the earth behind it flows down some great opening into the Underworld, for after all these years the gorge has never filled up, neither does any of the water flow back again."

"Maybe this is so, my son," said the Kikmonwi gravely, "but it may be that it travels so great a distance that the lives of many old men would be too short to follow it."

"Be that so or not, I must go and solve this mystery, Inaa, for I can find no peace in my mind until I do so," insisted Tiyo firmly.

Then his father took out his ancient stone pipe and smoked and smoked, while he searched his wisdom for the best way to help his son in this perilous undertaking upon which he was determined.

At last he spoke: "It is impossible for you to follow the river on foot, hence we must look for a hollow cottonwood tree, and I will show you how to make a winacibuh, in which you may float safely upon the waters of the Far-Far-Below River."

Eagerly did Tiyo search until he found such a tree, and the girth of it was such that it took the outstretched arms of the old Kikmonwi and his son's to span it. This they felled and cut from it a section as long as the body of the youth. Then, with stone ax and living embers, they gouged and burned out all of the inside, leaving only a thin shell like a huge drum. Small branches and twigs were then fitted into one of the open ends so as to close it completely, and the interstices were pitched thoroughly with pinyon gum.

At last all was done and his father looked upon Tiyo sadly. "After four sleeps, Itii (my son), you may start upon your journey. Your mother and sisters will make you kwipdosi from husked corn, boiled and dried and ground, while I with prayer and fasting will make you such pahos as I know you will need to win favor from those you will encounter on your journey."

When the morning of the fifth day had come Tiyo was chafing and straining to be on his way, so his father brought to him the prayer sticks and explained to him their meaning and their uses. Carefully he placed them on a fresh white cotton mantle—"This is Wupo Paho for Spider Woman; this for Hicanavaiya; this for Woman of the Hard Substances; this for Tawa, himself, may it please him; while the last is for the Muiyinwuh, the Germ God." Beside these magic tokens he laid a small quantity of fluffy white down from the eagle's thigh. "This is kwapuha, my son. The greatest magic lies in these trembling breath feathers, and Spider Woman will show you how to use it. I beg you that you walk carefully, for if you step amiss and offend one of these great ones it will go ill with you. Wrap all of these things in this mantle and see that you guard them with greatest care."

Then his mother, as is the way with women-folk, came forward with streaming eyes. Gently she handed him a tcakapta, and inside this food basin she had with cunning painted the sign of

Spider Woman, while on the outer surface was the symbol of Tawa. Cunning magic! To this gift she and each of Tiyo's sisters added shallow circular trays of coiled grass wrapped about with yucca shreds and heaped generously with the kwipdosi they had made him.

Now all was ready, and Tiyo crept into his timber-box. After handing the youth a stout pole of honwi wood with which to guide his craft, the Kikmonwi reluctantly but with greatest care closed the open end of the winacibuh, gave it a mighty heave and away it floated, bobbing up and down on the rushing waters of the Far-Far-Below River.

Through a small circular opening that had been left for the purpose, Tiyo thrust forth his pole, pushing away from the rocks that lay in the way of his craft. On he floated over smooth waters, sped madly through swift, rushing torrents, plunged down cataracts, and for many hours spun through wild whirlpools where black rocks thrust forth their heads like angry bears. At times when the spray dashed through the small opening Tiyo caught it in his basin to quench his thirst or to mix with his kwipdosi for gruel, but when the roaring waters came about his timber-box he closed the opening with a plug.

Tossed and buffetted by whirlpool and rapid, Tiyo continued on. The journey was fearsome enough to daunt the staunchest heart, but through it all Tiyo remained undaunted and eager for his task.

Tiyo Meets Spider Woman

A SUDDEN VIOLENT JOLT, then that motionlessness that meant the winacibuh had come to a rest. Tiyo's heart leapt with such violence that his ears sang like small drums, and he swiftly tore himself an opening in the timber-box. When he peered through the opening he saw that he had come up against a sandy shore. No live thing could he see, but to his alert ears seemed to come a sibilant "hsss, hsss." Taking his paho mantle in one hand he sprang out expectantly upon the stretch of sand. The hissing became louder, and he saw that it came from a small hole near his feet. Then the "hsss" sounded distinctly four times, so he bent a listening ear close above it, and a voice issued from the depths.

"Um pituh, you have arrived," came in true Hopi greeting. "My heart is glad. I have been long expecting you, Tiyo. Come into the house of Kokyanwuhti."

Kokyanwuhti! How the heart of Tiyo thrilled at the name—Kokyanwuhti, the great Spider Woman.

"Alas, how can I come to you," cried the perplexed Tiyo, "I have looked on every side and see only this tiny hole through which your voice comes, and it will scarce admit the point of my great toe."

"Come," was the abrupt command.

So Tiyo, without further question, placed his foot upon the hole; then, as if stirred to life, the

[15]

tiny particles of sand began to whirl about and in a marvellous way the opening widened until it allowed the admission of his body as he was drawn gently downwards. When his feet touched solid rock he pressed impetuously forward in a dim passageway until he found himself in a great stone kiva. Then before his eager eyes appeared the Mighty One, she of whom since infancy he had heard with bated breath—Spider Woman.

Now, though Spider Woman is as old as time, she is likewise as young as eternity, for she is Earth Mother, so Tiyo, feeling the endless youth of her, hailed her "Kokyamana," Spider Maid, and in the way of woman she was pleased with the stripling's flattering tribute. Encouraged by her smile, he eagerly unrolled his mantle and reverently handed her the Wupo Paho and the trembling breath feathers of eagle down.

"Ah," cried she with pleasure as she scanned the prayer stick with care, "this was made by One Who Knows. I thank you. I can be seen or I can become as air; I go everywhere and I know all things; I know from whence you come and whither you are bound; I know your heart is good; I know the things you want. I have prepared food for you—partake of it," and she set before him two cornmeal dumplings that magically increased as he ate them, so that, though they were very small when he started, he ate and was filled to the chin.

For four days the youth stayed in the kiva of Spider Woman, listening to her words of wisdom, while she compounded the magic medicine

[16]

that pacifies the snake and all angry animals. On the fifth day she gave it to him with these words, "Only the fearless can use this nahu; you keep your heart brave. There are Angry Ones who guard the kiva entrances to which you will go. You put this on the tip of your tongue and spurt it on such angry ones. You will see! They will become gentle as the rabbit. I will make myself small and sit behind your left ear so as to tell you what to do. See that your ears are keen and that you obey, or I shall leave you. Now take this down of Kwahu on your hand and step upon the sipapu over there."

Unquestioningly Tiyo obeyed his mentor, and as soon as he had done so the orifice opened just as before and he sank into the Underworld. When he came to a stop he stood waiting with his hand, upon which lay the eagle's down, out-stretched before him. A miracle! Slowly the feathers stirred as if alive, rose gently and floated toward the northwest. With his eyes fixed upon it, Tiyo followed eagerly until he came to where the projecting ends of a ladder gave evidence of a kiva below. But alas! this entrance was guarded by a most fearsome monster. It was no less a one than the great Snake, Gatoya, himself. His gray body was only so long as the youth's arm, but its girth was that of a man's body. Two large eyes gleamed from a multi-colored head and, from a venomous mouth that could breathe death to a long distance, projected two great teeth capable of piercing the thickest buckskin. Here was his way barred by the Guardian of All Angry Snakes.

[17]

Tiyo did not blanch, and, because fear had not entered his heart to becloud his mind, he remembered the words of Spider Woman and put the nahu upon the tip of his tongue. As the hideous reptile reared to strike viciously with his poisonous fangs, Tiyo spurted the charm upon it just in time, and it drooped its ugly head meekly and allowed the youth to pass. He exulted over the danger passed, and more he would gladly meet if he could only gain for his people the gift of more abundant rain. But, as he passed on, there sprang before his startled eyes two angry bears, growling and reaching toward him with violent claws. The nahu, however, was ready on his tongue so that when he spurted it at them they bowed their shaggy heads submissively, allowing him to descend the ladder unmolested.

What a strange sight now met his eyes! He entered a great gray stone kiva, the walls, the roof and floors of which were hung and covered with snakeskins. Stranger still were figures— half man, half reptile—that squatted around a sand ponya on the floor. None spoke or seemed to notice him. And there was the stillness of death in the gloom.

Then came the welcome voice of Spider Woman whispering softly in his ear, "These are the Ancestors, show one of your paho." When Tiyo displayed a paho, an old chieftain merely bent his head and silently motioned to a sipapu which led still lower.

As he descended through this, a very different sight gladdened both his eyes and heart.

Everything before him was light and cheerful, and many men sat around a brilliantly colored sand ponya chanting their songs to a low humming rhythm of many gourd rattles. Their garments and feather plumes were brightly colored, and from all came glad cries of welcome.

"You are now in Tchutcub kiva, the chamber of the Snake-Antelopes. Yonder chieftain is Hicanavaiya, Ancient of Six," whispered Spider Woman, who was now in the form of a tiny spider resting behind Tiyo's ear. "There stand the two beautiful daughters of the chief."

Standing on each side of the altar two maidens of wondrous grace and fairness of form caught Tiyo's attention. Both faces held his admiring eyes, but one held his gaze the longest, for she seemed as beautiful as the earth in its springtime unfoldment. It was with difficulty that he forced his eyes away from her face and turned to deliver the first Blue Paho to Hicanavaiya.

The chieftain looked at it very carefully before placing it by the sand ponya. "Now this is good," he said. "I can see that it was made by One Who Knows. I have been expecting you, and I thank you for coming. I cause the rain clouds to come and go. I cause the ripening winds to blow. 'Tis I who direct the coming and going of all mountain animals. Before you return to your home you will desire many things. Ask freely of me and you will receive, because your heart is good."

Tiyo would have been glad to tarry here in

the home of the lovely maiden, but Spider Woman bade him resume his journey. Difficult though it was to leave, he did not hesitate in his obedience. Reluctantly he tore his eyes from the maiden and passed onward up the hatchway. At this point the eagle down floated toward the west, and he knew that he must follow in that direction though it seemed to lead only to a vast stretch of water. All the waters of the world must be here, like the Endless Waters of First Tale. Undoubtedly this must be the place to which the Far-Far-Below River journeyed. Far out he could see the long tips of a ladder projecting above the shimmering waters. There seemed no way to proceed, so he had stopped at the very brink.

The voice of Spider Woman came softly: "Behold the House of Huzruiwuhti before you. It is on dry land that floats upon the surface of this great water. Take some kwapuha (eagle down), spurt some of the nahu (medicine) upon it, and cast it before you on the water."

When Tiyo did this, the water drew back on this hand and on that, so that a dry path appeared which enabled him to travel dry-shod to the distant ladder ends. He was just about to place his foot on the ladder when two angry puma appeared, glaring, snarling and baring their teeth. It had gone ill with him had he not leapt lithely back as he blew upon them the magic nahu. In a most amazing manner they became humble and subdued. Hanging their heads meekly, they said, "Never before have we permitted any human being to pass us alive. But we can see your breath is pure and your heart is brave." As they lay down, one on each side of the entrance, he stepped fearlessly between them and descended the ladder.

Like no other ladder he had ever seen was this one down which he made his way into the kiva of the Woman of the Hard Substances. Skillfully was its framework overlaid with an ornate decoration of iridescent white shells from the Land of the Far Waters. The kiva walls were likewise resplendent with shell and turquoise. In jarring contrast to all this beauty was the huddled figure of an ancient crone wrapped in a shabby mantle of dingy gray. Scant snow locks of extreme age framed her face—lined as deeply as the age-old, storm-beaten rock face of Pisisbaiya (Colorado River)—from which her dim eyes peered at the intruders.

Tiyo Travels Through the Underworld

"YOU ARE THINKING that you see an old woman, my Tiyo," whispered Spider Woman, "but judge not by the eye. There sits she who each day runs the whole course of her life, Huzruiwuhti. In her lord's absence she is as you now see her, withered and old, but every night upon his return she lays aside her drab mantle and becomes an enchanting maiden. At dawn she is clothed with radiant splendor, for here she lives with her always-bridegroom, Tawa.

[21]

Besides being beautiful, she is kind, and her heart is tender and generous."

So Tiyo paid the crone the reverence due the aged, and gently put into her hand the second Blue Paho. Holding it close to her dim eyes, she gave it the most intense scrutiny. At length a slow smile flickered over her shrivelled visage and she murmured: "Yes, this was made by One Who Knows. I thank you. Sit down and eat, and you may ask any of my possessions that your heart desires."

Then she placed before him a bowl of purest turquois and began mixing in it an enchanted food of corn pollen, saying as she performed the rite, "This will be ready for you and the Father when he comes, that you may both eat of it and start away without delay."

There came a low injunction from Spider Woman, "Hold in readiness for Tawa." The words had scarcely entered Tiyo's ear when the air seemed to grow warmer, and there came the sound of a mighty rushing in the air above. Suddenly, with a crash as that of a terrific lightning bolt, something landed on the roof above.

Tawa, the Sun! As he descended, his shining beauty poised upon the glittering ladder was almost too great for mortal eye to bear. The white buckskin of his garment shone like unsullied snow, and on the sleeves and leggings hung a deep fringe of jingling white shells. While the youth gazed with wide-eyed awe, Tawa hung up the shining shield he carried on his arm, and as it glanced against the stone wall it sang out ching-a-ling and rained down a shower of golden sparks.

The garment of Tawa was thick, being fashioned for the intense cold of the Above, and it was hung about with great pockets. From these Tawa drew forth great numbers of pahos that he had collected from shrines he had visited on his daily journey and laid them before Huzrui-wuhti. She was no longer the gray crone but stood slender and straight — a lovely maiden — before her lord. Then she began to sort them, laying some on her left hand, others on her right. The latter she gathered to her with a warm smile, "These are from ones having good hearts. I will send them all they ask." Then her face became stern and she pushed the pahos on the left away from her. "But these are from liars and deceitful men. My eyes are offended at their sight."

From his right wrist Tawa took some scalps, and they were from those who had been slain on the right side of his path during the day; then from his left wrist he removed others, and they were of those who had been slain on the left side of his path. Over these the maid rocked her body, weeping and moaning bitterly over the gory locks. "I grieve when you are brought to me; it stabs me with pain as I touch you. My heart is sad and I tremble as I look upon your frightfulness. Oh, my people, my people, why can you not live in peace? Will you never cease to rend my heart with your quarrelling," and she arose with sad face to hang the scalps against the beautiful turquoise walls.

[23]

Then it was that Tawa turned to Tiyo. "Who are you?" he asked.

"Yes," answered Tiyo, "I have come from way over there by the cliffs at Tokonabi. I have brought you something. My father made it and told me to give it to you," and he handed Tawa the third Blue Paho. "We haven't enough rain over there. The Far-Far-Below River takes it all away, or else the Rainbow comes out and eats up the water when it tries to rain. How about this? Is that great water outside this kiva that which the river drags away from the earth, and may not some of it be spared for my people? Our corn sickens and dies, our people hunger and Masauwuh is always prowling near us."

"So that is what you have been thinking about. I have been seeing you there on the cliffs watching the Far-Far-Below River." As he talked, Tawa was turning the paho over in his hands, examining it closely, but at last a gratified look overspread his features and he nodded graciously. "It is well, my relative, my son. This was made by One Who Knows. Let us smoke together."

He filled the pipe with sweet native tobacco, and the two smoked together long and silently. When this ceremony was finished they partook of the magic pollen food that Huzruiwuhti had prepared for them. "Now we will make a journey through the Below across to the place where I start again tomorrow. Put your hand upon my girdle and see to it that your hold is firm."

Tiyo's strong young fingers had no sooner

taken hold than with lightning swiftness they shot through the sipapu and started down to the house of the Germ God, Muiyinwuh, in the lowest depths of the Underworld. Down, down, down, they plunged their blazing way. As they neared their destination the air grew humid, and so vibrantly did it pulse with life that the heart of Tiyo beat with strange longings that put forth like green corn shoots in the spring. At the same time, with strangest magic did a vision of the Snake Maiden appear before his eyes.

"Here are we at the house of Muiyinwuh," said Tawa, leading him through a host of busy little men who swarmed to and fro like bees, working with eager haste. "Now you can see how it is done in this place. The life of all things starts here."

"So, you have come," said Muiyinwuh as he approached.

"Yes, I have brought you this Cakwa Paho. My father made it over there in Tokonabi," said Tiyo, placing the last blue paho in the god's hand.

"Yes, this was made by One Who Knows," declared Muiyinwuh nodding his head above it sagely. "Because of this I will always listen to the wishes of your people when they make it this way. At my word the life of all things starts — the seed of all green things that grow upon the face of the earth, the life of every animal and of all men. These creatures you see, they are always working at this task. They will always be working thus."

With wonder Tiyo looked upon these things, and he noted that the largest, finest workers were the most earnest and industrious, while the poor, wizened creatures were shiftless and indifferent. All about him life seemed to be pulsing like some gigantic heart, and Tiyo felt coursing through his being a mighty desire to accomplish great things and the ability to do so. Again Muiyinwuh gave the youth the most earnest assurances of his good will toward him and all of his people.

Tawa now motioned toward his red horsehair girdle, and Tiyo grasped it firmly as he had before. So, with a wave of farewell to Muiyinwuh, they started forth for the place where the sun arises. No stop was made until they came to Tawaki, Sun House of the East, and though it had seemed that no place could equal in beauty that of the Sun's western kiva, here beauty so resplendent met Tiyo's eyes that he could not decide which was the greater. Instead of blue, every shade of red and pink glowed, and they ate their food from a polished stone bowl that looked like the upturned rosy sky at dawn.

There was no woman in this kiva; Tawa and his brother Taiowa occupied it alternately. For four days Tawa carried the burnished shield across the heavens, returning each night to the kiva of Huzruiwuhti; thence through the Underworld, reaching the Above just in time to march across its blue arch. Then, while he rested in his beautiful rose kiva, Taiowa, whom he had created to relieve him, carried the shield for four days' time.

As they rested there, Tawa gave Tiyo wise counsel, bidding him be grateful that his desire to know the great mysteries had been granted and impressing upon him the importance of cherishing, not only the things he had already learned, but those yet to be revealed. As he talked, he showed him how to make the Great Sun Paho.

"When you have learned this magic your eyes will be opened, and for all time you will know all people; you will be able to look into their hearts; you will be able to read their thoughts," he promised. And, of a truth, when Tiyo had learned to make this paho he could hear his family mourning for him and calling upon him to return. His heart so yearned over their sorrow that had it not been that he had not yet won from the gods the promise of more abundant rains and that the face of the Snake Maid beckoned him, he would have returned at once to comfort them.

Tawa smiled, seeing into the heart of the youth. "Do not falter, my son. I counsel you that of all the gifts you will receive the one you will most prize will be the Rain Cloud, which you will receive at the hands of the chief of the Snake-Antelope kiva." Then Tawa gave him the skin of Gray Fox to hang upon the hatchway of the kiva, and when he had hung it upon the hatchway of the kiva it brought upon the White Dawn. The next day Tawa handed him the skin of Sikyataiyo, Yellow Fox, to hang over the gray skin and, behold, the Yellow Dawn appeared. This was most potent magic.

All had now been done, and Tawa was ready to leave Tawaki; but this time he took the youth upon his shoulder and, carrying him across the sky's blue dome, showed him all the world with its wonders outspread far below like a marvellously woven blanket. When, at sunset, they came to the House in the West, Huzruiwuhti brought forth gifts of all that was in the house — shell, turquoise and coral — saying, "Now you will leave me: Take these gifts!"

Gratefully Tiyo murmured "Kwakwai, kwakwai," as he wrapped them in his white cotton mantle. He turned to say farewell, and lo! he beheld the miracle of transformation with his own eyes. As Tawa approached the old woman, the decrepit female figure seemed to dissolve, as does gray mist before the morning sun, and, radiantly emerging, stood a beautiful maiden who awaited her lord with outspread arms.

At the top of the ladder Tiyo found himself again gazing at the shimmering waters that surrounded the kiva, but after a moment's pause he remembered what he must do. So, upon a remaining bit of eagle's down, he spurted the nahu and cast it upon the waters. As before, they rolled back to the right hand and to the left and so stayed, leaving him a dry path upon which to proceed. The golden glow of evening flooded everything. Far away he could see the projecting ends of the ladder that led down into the Snake-Antelope kiva, and hanging upon them was the red-fringed warrior's bow that betokened secret ceremonials below.

[28]

Tiyo Appears Before Snake Mana

FOUR SLEEPS HAVE PASSED since you were last here, my Tiyo," said Spider Woman, "and what wonders you have seen and heard in that time. Now you are to go down here and receive the greatest blessing of all."

So this time, without challenge, Tiyo descended into the kiva of the Snake-Antelope priests. More wonderful to him than all the brilliance of Tawa's brazen shield was the light that leapt into the eyes of the Snake Mana when he appeared before her.

For four days Tiyo sat beside the sand ponya of this priesthood as one of them. He learned how to make this ponya with solemn ritual. It was rectangular in shape and outlined by a band of fine white sand; within this border were bands of red, green and yellow sand, separated each from the other by fine lines of black. The four sides represented the Four World Quarters, and the colors were those of the corn. Inside these bands was a field of white sand upon which were four sets of semicircles in the same colors, which represented rain clouds, while the parallel black lines running at right angles to them were rain. From between the set of white rain clouds lay four zigzag bands in the same four colors, outlined in black, and these were the snake symbols for lightning. Each snake had a horn on his triangular head, and each one wore a necklace. Set all about this altar were many magic ornaments and fetishes, and only those who had been tried and found both wise and good were permitted to sit beside it and learn its secrets.

While Tiyo sat here he listened to the wisdom of Hicanavaiya; he sang his songs, he intoned his prayers, and as he did so he learned to make pahos that would bring the rain and were known to these priests alone. "Here we have an abundance of rain and corn," Hicanavaiya told him, "while in your mesa land there is little of either, so thus shall you use your nahu. Fasten these prayers in your breast; these songs shall you sing and these prayers shall you make. Then, when you have painted your body in black and white bands as I have shown you, with the symbols of the snake, the clouds will come."

Then he gave Tiyo a part of everything that was in the two kivas, the bright one gay with feathers and the gloomy one hung with snake-skins. From the Snake-Antelope kiva he gave him all the colors of the sand so that he could make an altar of his own at Tokonabi. And because the youth had become learned in all this magic lore, the heart of the old chief was warm toward him as toward his own son, and he bound about his slim loins the woven white kilt of the Snake-Antelopes. When this had been done he caused the heart of the youth to leap like the mountain goat, for he waved his hand toward his two daughters saying:

"Here are the two mana who know the charm that prevents death from the bite of the rattlesnake. Take them with you also. The one toward whom your heart is soft is Tcuamana; take her for your wife. That other one you are to give to your younger brother, and she will become the mother of the Flute clan." When Tiyo turned to take this most precious gift, behold! he saw that both maids were enveloped about with fleecy clouds, like a mantle, which made them even more beautiful.

Now, with solemn mien, Hicanavaiya took a feathered object from beside the ponya. It was the sacred tiponi, the Snake chieftain's most precious emblem of office. Placing it most reverently in Tiyo's arms, he charged him solemnly to cherish it always with most jealous care.

"Truly, this is your mother, for it is made from the corn that nourishes the Good People." Then from the ponya he took another tiponi. "This is for your younger brother. See that he treasures it."

When Tiyo had put these with his other treasures in the white mantle, the chief gave to him these last words of wisdom: "See that you remember all you have heard and seen, and all that I have done, do you the same. Take my heart and my bowels and all my thoughts; then shall you become the father of a great clan and shall be called by my name."

So Tiyo bade him farewell, and as he stepped forth lithe, straight and good to look upon in the strength of his young manhood, the two daughters of Hicanavaiya followed behind him. The tiny magic spider still whispered into his left ear directions back to her kiva, from which his journey through the underworld had so lately started.

For four days he stayed there, hunting rabbits for her, while Spider Woman with cunning fingers wove him a hoapuh, a deep basket pannier with rounded ends, made of interlaced wicker strands, for him to carry on his back. When she had completed it, even to the fastening of a cotton cord upon it, she bade him farewell. "My Tiyo, thou hast learned all the secrets of the Four World Quarters and the Above and Below. Shut in thy heart all this wisdom, revealing it only to those whose hearts you have tried and found perfect."

Then she bade Tiyo get into the pannier, with a maiden on each side of him, and she disappeared up the hatchway. The three waited breathless, not knowing which way to turn next; then they beheld, slowly unwinding through the sipapu, a silvery filament. With fascinated eyes they watched the silvery spider line uncoil, swaying and shimmering — nearer and nearer, until at last it began like a live thing to wind itself around the cotton cord of the hoapuh.

The hoapuh stirred. It moved gently but irresistibly as an unseen force lifted it through the hatchway. Up, up and up, until it reached the white, fleecy clouds of the vast Above. Like some gigantic bird it sailed with them, following the silver thread of the Far-Far-Below River, until at last it hung over the rocky cliffs of Tokonabi. Then Spider Woman spun out the gossamer

[32]

thread, and gently the hoapuh lowered to the ground. But as they neared the ground they could see the people fleeing in terror to their houses, or to any rock that might afford a shelter. Shrill cries of "Kwataka, Kwataka" floated to them, and Tiyo, knowing their thoughts, saw that his people had taken the hoapuh for some huge bird hovering aloft. Nay, they thought it was the dread Man-Eagle himself come to harass them. So, laughing mightily, he called out in a big voice for them to come forth and welcome him home.

Tiyo Returns Home

AT TIYO'S SHOUT of reassurance the people of Tokonabi crept fearfully forth from their hastily sought shelters, and when they saw that it was really their own Tiyo who had returned to them after so strange a fashion, they crowded about him, eager to make him welcome and listen breathlessly to his thrilling account of his travels through the Underworld.

Then Tiyo led the Snake Maidens to the house of his mother where they were to remain four days, unseen by anyone, grinding corn into fine meal, according to the marriage custom. Tiyo and his younger brother now called together all the male relatives to help them prepare wedding gifts for the brides. They wove two blue, cotton tunic robes, two white blankets bordered with red and black and having elaborate tassels at the corners, and long-fringed girdles to bind about the tunics. They also made moccasins, each pair having leggings that took half a deerskin in the making. For this outfit they made reed mats in which to keep them.

On the fifth day after their return Tiyo mounted to a housetop, as does the Speaker Chief, and proclaimed loudly:

"Hear, oh my people, men of Tokonabi! Back from my travels have come two strange mana, daughters of Hicanavaiya, the Ancient of Six. One of them I shall take to wife, the other is espoused to my brother, and from henceforth they will abide with us and be one with us. In sixteen days' time we will make their feast as it is meet we should do when a strange people comes among us.

"While at the House of the Rising Sun my eyes were opened, and it was given to me henceforth to know the mysteries and to know the hearts of all men. So now, ye men of Tokonabi, make ye ready, make ye ready, for it is my purpose to try you, and those among you whose hearts I find perfect shall be my priests and my brothers. These I shall teach new pahos, as I have been taught them, and you shall learn the prayers and sing the songs that Hicanavaiya gave me to carry in my breast. My heart that knows not fear shall be yours, my bowels and all my thoughts. In my kiva you shall be initiated into all those secret rites that will make the Rain

Cloud do our bidding, and you will be priests of the Snake-Antelopes."

So all the men of Tokonabi set about making their hearts perfect and searching their thoughts that they might go before Tiyo for their test of worthiness.

Then the heads of both brides and grooms were washed in yucca suds by the mother of Tiyo, according to Hopi marriage custom. Upon the bride of Tiyo was placed a white blanket girt about with one of the long-fringed girdles. Her hair was brushed until its midnight hue took on the lustre of starlight; it was looped low over her ears and bound at the back. Over her rounded red-bronze shoulders a second white mantle was draped and upon this were tied feathers, one upon each shoulder and two in back over her shoulder blades. A white feather from the altar of her fathers was bound against her hair, and two large shell earrings hung from her ears.

Truly, Tiyo thought he had never seen anything more fair than this mana, when his mother gave her to him, and he led her proudly to her house that would henceforth be known as the Snake-Antelope House. And with the other brother went the other maid in her wedding finery to the Flute kiva.

Four times did Tawa and his brother Taiowa alternate in carrying the sun shield across the skies, and when the sixteenth day had passed the great feast for the Tcuamana commenced. Upon the fifth day of the feast low clouds trailed over Tokonabi, and from a rainbow descended a vast host of Snake people from the Underworld to do honor to their kinswoman. But, after they had been taken to the kiva for the feasting, they would eat nothing but corn pollen, and suddenly disappeared. For the next three days Tokonabi was overhung with the same lowering clouds, and upon each evening fresh hosts of Snake people from the Underworld descended from the rainbow, and, after partaking of nothing more than corn pollen, disappeared as the first visitors had.

On the morning of the ninth day a strange thing happened. When the Tokonabi men went forth into their valleys they found that their unearthly visitants had been transformed into venomous reptiles, and they knew not what to do. Therefore, they reproached Tiyo for the evil magic he had brought among them. Then the Tcuamana spoke to them, "We understand this; let the Younger Brothers go out and bring all these our people in. Then must you wash their heads and let them dance with you."

This seemed a most dangerous thing to do, but Tiyo reminded them that the Tcuamana knew the nahu that prevents death from rattlesnake bite. So they went forth unafraid and gathered up the reptiles as they had been bid. Then, when they had washed the heads of the snakes in huge stone jars, the men of Tokonabi danced with the snakes they had gathered in from the valleys.

They danced thus till sunset when Tiyo made a house of snake meal and they carefully laid the snakes within. All the people came to it that they might cast prayer meal upon them. When this had been done the Younger Brothers, for thus were the new Snake priests called, gently raised the snakes and carried them back to the valleys. Then, lo! the strange visitants all disappeared, carrying with them the prayers and petitions of the people of Tokonabi. Strangest of all, they had hardly left when the black clouds gathered, the great fiery serpent of the skies appeared biting and bellowing and the rains descended in abundance.

So now Tiyo had accomplished all his heart had longed to do. His mind was rich in magic lore. The Rain Cloud would now do his bidding so that the corn would grow and his people thrive. His heart sang at the sight of the Tcuamana who so ably cooked his food or busied her fingers in basket weaving or in modelling the yellow clay into vessels and decorating them with cunning designs in red and black. Truly it had gone well with him because he had kept his thought high and his heart unafraid.

Tiyo Rejoins His Clan

THERE CAME A DAY when blankets were spread across the usually wide open doors of Tiyo and his brother, while feeble cries issuing forth betokened that the Tcuamana had given birth to offspring, and the tribe rejoiced in the good fortune of their hero, Tiyo. But imagine their horror when they went in to see the newborn to find them strange creatures, more snake than human. Then, alas, later when the children of Tokonabi came in to play with them, the strange creatures bit them venomously and the children died.

A great weeping arose from the bereaved mothers of Tokonabi, and they demanded of their husbands that they lead them and their remaining children away to new homes, leaving Tokonabi to the Tcuamana and their strange offspring. In truth there seemed nothing else to do but abandon their homes and journey forth into the Unknown. Now this required great courage, for in those days of the earth's childhood many monsters of celestial origin, most of whom were hostile to mankind, roamed abroad, infesting both earth and sky and particularly harassing the Hopi. But Tiyo had given them his heart that knew not fear and often in extremity they had been given timely help by Spider Woman and the Twins, the Youth and the Echo. So they made a ceremony to bring rain that they might follow in its wake across the semi-arid country that lay all about them, and they set forth.

At first the Puma, the Sand and the Horn people started southward together, but after a short time the Horn people left and the Puma journeyed on to Wukoki, where they built themselves a village. With them dwelt one of the Tcamahia, but he, too, left them, travelling off to the southeast looking for other people who, he said, were coming up from the Underworld. Word came back to them that he journeyed on until he came upon the Twin, the Youth. "I can find those people for you," said the Twin confidently and fitting his arrow fletched with the bluebird's wing to the bow he shot it into the sky.

They watched it skim away like a tireless bird until it disappeared from their sight. Far to the northeast it fell, close to a sipapu from which new people were still climbing. In wonderment these people looked at the magic arrow, shaking their heads and saying, "There must be other people already here."

To their further amazement the arrow replied, "Yes, there are many people here, the Puma, the Horn, the Sand and others. I am from the bow of the Little War God, the Youth, who shot me here to find out about you for one of the Tcamahia. Now I will go back and tell him where you are." Whereupon the arrow soared back to the Youth so that the Tcamahia could journey forth to make them welcome.

All this time the rest had stayed at Wukoki, but now, inspired by the success of the Tcamahia, they set out and finally halted at a little spring in the middle mesa. Looking all about them, they could see no people in all the land about, yet most strangely, when night fell they beheld a fire that moved back and forth along the base of the mesa. From the gap to the point it moved back and forth, and they did not

[39]

know what to think about it. They thought they had better find out more about the thing before going farther, so they called on Mourning Dove to find out the cause of this fire, just as he had spied out springs for their fathers. His sharp eyes soon caught sight of monstrous tracks of bare feet upon the ground. Tirelessly he followed the huge tracks around in the great circle they made, encompassing the Place of Snow Peaks on the west, Red River on the south, Great River on the east, and the San Juan on the north. Mourning Dove knew that these tracks could have been made by no other than the dread Masauwuh himself, god of war and death. Quite terrified, he flew back to tell the people. Here was Something! And Tiyo, who had dealt with so many of the Mighty Ones, was not here to advise them.

As for Tiyo, he had been very sad at what had befallen his people through the strange offspring, sadder still when they had left Tokonabi. Finally after long thinking he said to the Tcuamana, "I think it would be well if we would take our strange children back to your people, for truly they are out of place here. Then we may seek out my people and stay with them, for did not Hicanavaiya say that I was to be the father of a great tribe?" So she consented and Tiyo made paho, and taking the little snake creatures he made the journey back to the Snake-Antelope kiva in the Underworld. When he had told his wife's people all that had happened they agreed that it would be best to leave them there, and Tiyo returned to his wife.

Then Tiyo and the Tcuamana travelled south-eastward until they at last saw smoke in the distance, and as they neared it they could see a village perched on the rocks of the mesa, looking like a part of the native rocks. Now this village was that which had been built by his clan when they had halted at the foothills of the mesa when Mourning Dove had told them of the great footsteps of Masauwuh that encompassed them. They had named this place Walpi, the Place Near the Gap. Tiyo drew near and called out to those within the village.

"I have come with my wife and I wish to live with you again and be your father."

At first the people were reluctant to admit them, but when they were assured that the little snakes had been returned to the Underworld they gladly consented, for they all wanted Tiyo to do something about the monster Masauwuh. For a long time they saw no more of Masauwuh than his mighty tracks, but they suffered so from fear that Tiyo decided that the monster must be faced. He called to him all his bravest men and asked that they go with him to meet the Death God, reminding them that their hearts were without fear.

Halfway to the middle mesa they met him, and the sight was so gruesome as to make the eyes strain from their sockets. Had not their hearts been staunch they would have turned back, for he was hideous beyond words. Raw flesh and clots of blood hung all over his body, and his great head was ugly and glaring. Tiyo strode fearlessly in front of the rest and challenged him.

"Come forward to meet me if you dare. You are not good and we do not want you. We are the Peaceful People and we do not want to serve a war god. My heart is strong and I will overcome you."

With that the two rushed forward and grappled with each other. Long and mightily did they battle, wrestling until they churned up the ground in hollows. But finally Tiyo embraced the monster so strongly in his strong, young arms that Masauwuh was overcome.

Then, acknowledging Tiyo's great valor, Masauwuh spoke out fairly to him. "I see you are someone. I see you are strong of heart. I had designed to kill you all if your hearts had not been good; now I am satisfied. Sit down."

At this Masauwuh removed the hideous head, and it was seen to be a mask, and, underneath, his face was seen to be that of a handsome youth. Then he sat upon the mask and solemnly brought forth his pipe, and when they had seated themselves in a circle about him he graciously passed it to each man and they smoked together. When this ceremony was over he looked upon them with kindly eye, saying in his deep, slow voice: "I also, am large of heart; all this land has been mine, but now all that lies within the limits of my footsteps shall be yours, because you have met me unafraid. But you must make me paho and offer them to me as you do to the other gods. There is my house and there you shall put my paho." He pointed out a rocky spot close to the west side of the mesa and they agreed to do as he bade.

When they turned back to him he had vanished, but over on the rocky west side of the mesa stood his altar, and all about them, bounded by his huge naked footprints, lay the land that Tiyo had won for them by his fearless heart.

So within these boundaries Tiyo settled down to live with his clan, to follow what was good and live in peace. In time there were born to him and the Tcuamana other children, and they were not like the first little monsters. So they continued to make the prayers and sing the songs that Tiyo brought them, along with the Rain Cloud, from the Underworld — and so do their children's children continue to do even unto this day. Even today do the Snake priests dance with their brothers from the Underworld and compel the Rain Cloud to do their bidding.

The Youth Who Brought the Corn

TIME WAS WHEN THE ANCIENT PEOPLE had dwelt in a wonderful land in which there was an abundance of rain and the corn was lusty and plenteous. But they wandered forth from this paradise and found themselves in the Land of Little Rain where there was neither stream nor spring, though, to be sure, the uprooting of a tuft of grass revealed water just below the surface. Besides this, food was scarce for they had no seed for corn, squash, or other garden plants they needed. The gods, withholding their favors, seemed far off. Only Masauwuh was ever close because of the ever-threatening famine, and though they entreated him to be merciful and leave them he paid no attention but continued to skulk around their borders snatching whom he could.

One day when their despair had almost overcome them there appeared in their midst a little, wizened old man who was quite a stranger to them. Something about his very presence seemed to make their hearts less heavy and that, too, before he had spoken.

[44]

"Let not your hearts be faint, for despair is the strongest ally Masauwuh has. I have two sisters who are wives to the great Calako. Petition them—it may be that they will help you."

At once the hearts of all lightened with new hope, and they set about happily to build a new altar upon which to offer pahos to Calako. Each man wrought a paho, and they set them around a sand hillock so as to form a circle. But when they had performed their magic rites, not Calako but a brother of Masauwuh appeared.

"There is something you should know," he said to them. "Wherever Calako sets his feet a deep gorge appears. This is no proper altar for such a one. If you want Calako to come you must get a big rock for him to stand on," and without saying any more he vanished.

The people lost no time in following his advice, with great labor bringing a large stone to a place beside the altar for the god to stand on. On each side of the altar they placed paho made especially for the wives of Calako, to win their favor. Then each man put a paho for Calako on the altar and each stood before his own paho swinging a rattle rhythmically. Then there was silence. The men looked at each other blankly, for beyond this they knew not how to proceed— alas! they knew no magic song. Long they stood so, looking each at the other, each afraid to proceed with the ceremony for fear of doing something amiss.

As they stood mute, afraid to go on—afraid not to—a youth, too young to be even of full standing in the priesthood, stepped forward. Seizing the largest rattle, he shook it vigorously while his voice broke out in a song such as none of them had ever heard—a song loud, clear and unafraid. At this hardihood all hearts stood still, for they thought that not Masauwuh's brother but the Death God himself might appear. Then the heavy silence was broken by the sound of mighty rushing waters. Frightened eyes darting hither and thither could glimpse no sign of any water from which such a sound might proceed. Then burst upon their ears the sound of wild sweeping winds, yet when they looked about them not even the breath feathers on the pahos stirred in the motionless air. But looking at the great rock it was seen to be pierced through the center with a large hole, and it was through this that the strange sounds issued.

What had this rash youth done? What misfortune had his ignorance brought upon them? The men gazed at each other with terror-stricken eyes. Then with one impulse they turned and fled in wild panic—all save the youth who had sung the strange new song. Erect and fearless he stood awaiting whatever might be yet to follow. From the hole in the rock a voice now issued, and it sounded as though it were coming from the lowest cavity in the Underworld.

"I have heard your song. It was good. Let the bravest from among you come down and meet the Germ God."

"The bravest among them" when all save he had fled in terror! So the young man answered

[46]

him. "I am ready. What shall I do to enter the Underworld?"

"Place your hand upon the rock before you," returned the voice.

So the youth laid his hand upon the rock. First a mere cleft rayed off from the hole; then, as if alive, it enlarged until it was wide enough to permit the entrance of his body, and he made his way into the world below. At the end of the narrow passage he entered a room so beautiful that it dazzled his unaccustomed eyes, set about as it was with iridescent glimmer of shell, turquoise and coral. But from this his wondering eyes were drawn by a sight even more compelling. In the center of all this magnificence of color stood one he was sure was a divine being. The robes were resplendent and girt about the loins with a brilliant red, horsehair girdle. Upon one arm hung a shining brazen shield, but in his other hand there was nothing save a long, wicked-looking yucca whip.

As the youth approached he was greeted by the deity: "You are welcome here but you will have to endure much suffering before you leave. If you are brave of heart, however, you will be allowed to carry back to your people gifts of greatest value." By his own suffering he would bring blessing to his people. He did not hesitate and his face shone with high purpose as he made answer.

"That is all right. I am ready to go on with whatever you have for me."

"Kneel before me," came the curt command.

As the youth obeyed, the god raised the yucca whip high above his head and like a bolt of lightning the cruel whip descended upon the bare, smooth back of the youth, biting a red path across the quivering flesh. Stroke after stroke fell until the youth was almost spent from loss of blood and pain. But through all the swift torture no whimper escaped his close-locked lips, and his heart remained unshaken.

At last the ordeal was over, and the god led the youth over in front of his altar where his two wives stood one on each side. Stooping over, he chose a plumed paho from many others and handed it to the youth, explaining to him how he must use it. "Every year you must plant this prayer stick in the shrine you have built for me, and in reward I will bring you gifts from nature. From the youths of your clan you must choose those of proper age. Dressed like the Sun, you shall do to them as I have done to you, singing my songs and flogging them to test their bravery, as I have tested you. As a proof that I will aid you I will now give you this bundle of seeds to plant. Now put your hand on the rock above you."

As the youth obeyed his command, a passageway opened allowing him to return as he had come. Then the rock closed behind him, and though he put his hand upon it again and again it refused to open, but the print of his hand stayed upon it and remained there for all time that has come.

There was great joy among his friends and relatives when he rejoined them, but they looked with sad eyes at his raw flesh covered with splinters of yucca and willow. "That is but the price I have had to pay for those things I have brought back to you, my people, and I have paid it gladly. Because I stood his test, Calako himself became visible to me, and he has appointed me to be chief of his altar."

"Tell us how the great Calako looks," begged one.

"Alas, I cannot. His grandeur is too glorious to describe, but his wives are very beautiful. Would that you might see their splendid feather garments and the fine bordered blankets of white that hung from their shoulders. Upon their heads were terraced rain clouds; many kinds of flowers and jewels adorned them, besides every seed of corn such as they have sent us for food. There was white, red, yellow, blue and black; another kind was speckled red and yellow. Such colors! They were like precious stones."

At last they had heard the story of all the marvels he had seen and again stood fearful and wide-eyed as he strode to the great rock altar and shook his rattle above the rock. Hardly had he done so when a voice issued forth commanding, "Bring before my altar your finest young men that I may choose my priests."

The youth gathered together all the young men of proper age and brought them before the altar. "Now let them dip their hands in mixed water and earth and each make his imprint upon the rock. Those whose print dries instantly shall be my priests, because their hearts are not cold with fear."

Then the chosen youths were taken one by

one before the altar and flogged with yucca and willow. "Those who have made no outcry are my priests, forever," said the voice. "They shall take neither flesh nor salt for ten days; then will I return with my wives to teach them my songs and my prayers." At the appointed time all stood ready before the altar, and when the young Chief of the Altar shook his rattle a hole opened and the voice of Calako came forth as before. "I have come back with my wives to teach you the mysteries. See that you nourish them in your hearts and forget them not." So, after he had taught them all his songs and his prayers, there appeared in the hand of each youth five grains of all the different kinds of corn. "Plant one for the hot wind, one for the field rat, one for the kachina, and two for yourselves."

The wives of Calako now bade the women bring baskets of woven grass and place them around the altar. For a moment there was thick darkness; then behold they were seen to be filled with the seeds of squashes, melons and beans— all the vegetables that the Hopi have since possessed. The people who had so long fed upon wild things and had been so often near the clutches of Masauwuh could scarce believe their eyes, and they broke forth in wild songs of joy and thankgiving.

All was done. "I am leaving with you my masks and ceremonial robes, but I shall return again," said the voice of Calako, and as it ceased the hole closed and silence reigned.

The seeds were planted and all went well. The plants flourished and food became more plentiful, but Calako did not return as he had promised. The priests performed their services faithfully, but still the god was silent. Had they forgotten the songs? Fear almost took possession of their hearts lest they never hear him again. Suddenly, one day when the prayers were being intoned to the hum of many rattles, there appeared before their astonished eyes, not Calako, but a gigantic snake who wore upon his head a plume of feathers. It was Palulkon, the Great Plumed Serpent.

"Not by the mere singing of songs and shaking of rattles can you compel the return of Calako," said the Great Plumed Serpent. "He is only won by bravery, and, unless one of you is brave enough to return the masks and garments he left here, Calako and his wives will never return. But, if there is one brave enough to do this, you will actually see Calako himself. I have spoken."

Not one of the young priests but blenched at this proposal, for in the years that had passed since that first youth had brought them the corn they had become less brave and their hearts were not in their songs. So it was that at last the oldest man stepped forward, scornful of their cowardice, and offered to carry back the sacred masks and garments. No one was ever told how he got there or what happened, for he would say nothing.

Not long after the masks had been returned it seemed at last to please Calako to return; but instead of his presence bringing joy to the hearts of his priests they were rendered uneasy and fearful — the songs and prayers seemed strange, and they were sad and bewildered. Again and again some priest would stop and call out, "Someone is here whose heart is not good," or again, "Whose heart is bad?" But this did not uncover the trouble. Instead of prosperity, they fell into sore trouble, and at last the seed did not sprout and they knew they had offended Muiyinwuh, God of All Life Germs.

The people became desperate and famine ridden — what had they done amiss to fall into so great misfortune? At last a keen-eyed youth discovered that the supposed Calako carried a cedar branch in his hands, and his eyes were opened. This was no Calako at all but an imposter, for he knew that Calako always carried either yucca or willow. Then he knew that Masauwuh had in some way obtained the masks that they supposed had been returned to Calako. The Great Plumed Serpent must have betrayed them. Masauwuh carried the cedar bough; it must be he and his brothers who were masquerading in the stolen masks as Calako and his wives. No wonder things had gone amiss! What to do?

He determined that he would find a way to right the matter and prayed to the mighty Spider Woman to help him. Searching this way and that, at last he came upon Masauwuh fast asleep. Surely had Spider Woman delivered him into his hands. Cautiously he crept upon him, not breathing, not making a sound. With infinite care he began to recover the stolen garments that were strewn around the sleeping Death God. He would pull a bit, and if Masauwuh stirred so much as a breath feather he would desist. It took a long time and great courage and patience, but at last he succeeded in getting every bit of the sacred paraphernalia and made off with them with the swiftness of the deer.

With joy and thanksgiving the priesthood now returned to their sacred rites, determined to expiate the sin they had committed by having, even unwittingly, followed strange gods. At last, quite unexpectedly, as was his custom, Palulkon again appeared in the midst of their ceremonies.

"It is well with you mesa-folk again. Muiyinwuh is no longer angry and has sent me to tell you he has no further punishments for you since one of you was clever enough to discover the deception that you foolishly allowed to be practiced upon you. But be alert in the future. As for Calako, he will never appear before you. This youth who was brave enough to recover his masks and garments, he wishes to take his place and wear his masks. From this time on, whenever you have the proper number of eligible young men you shall make a feast to Calako, and it shall be called the Powamu. I have spoken."

So to this day in the Hopi pueblos the Powamu festival is made each year, and he who represents the great god Calako, dressed as the Sun, flogs the Hopi youth to test their bravery.

The Twins Visit Tawa

ON THE WEST SIDE OF MT. TAYLOR deep in her mysterious kiva of hoary gray stone, hung with floating drapery of dew-gemmed gossamer web, dwelt the all-powerful Spider Woman with her twin grandsons, Puukonhoya, the Youth, and Palunhoya, the Echo. There were none others like these, fine sturdy lads, quick and agile, fearful of nothing in the length and breadth of the earth they roamed so joyously. Why, not even that great giant Tcaveyo, himself, affrighted them, for did they not attack him alone and single-handed?

It happened after this fashion. They were at the Great Pool near their home when they saw him come there to slake his mighty thirst. Not content to do that, he furiously scattered to this side and to that the green painted prayer sticks with their dangling feathers that had been placed there to win the favor of the water gods. They beheld him kneel down and drink so deeply that four times the Great Pool was emptied—that Tcaveyo was someone! When he had drunk his fill he straightway lifted his ugly head to sniff the wind, immediately getting scent of the hiding

[54]

Twins. On the instant his weapon came hurtling at them through the air. Just as quickly, the twin in the path of the speeding weapon sprang into the air and, as it whizzed beneath him, caught it dexterously in his hand. Then, with a bellow, Tcaveyo flung his lightning, but the twin caught that as easily as he had the weapon. So then Puukonhoya flung his weapon at Tcaveyo, but it glanced harmlessly from the flint shirt that the monster always wore. Puukonhoya followed this by another terrific assault, but this only caused the great creature to stagger. Finally both the Twins threw the lightning that had been given them by their father, Tawa, and this knocked him down, killing him outright. Well were they called "the little but mighty ones."

Brought up as they had been upon tales about their mighty father, the Sun God, as they grew older they became consumed with the desire to visit him in his House in the West. And so they laid siege for their grandmother's permission to visit him, knowing full well that she would be loath to have them brave the dangers that lay between them and their father's kiva. So, first Puukonhoya would coax her, and when he had paused Palunhoya would take up the attack where his brother had left off. In due time Puukonhoya would relieve him, and so it went on until Kokyanwuhti yielded to their entreaties, not, however, without gravely warning them of the perils that lay before them.

"You will have to pass all the Fierce Guardians of his home, my children. These creatures

[55]

are dangerous beyond belief and keep a sleepless watch before his portals. Without a fearless heart and the most mighty magic anyone who attempts to pass them perishes miserably. Here is a strong nahu (medicine) of magic flour that I have made you. Guard it with your lives, and, when you approach the Fierce Guardians who oppose your progress, be quick to chew a bit of this meal and spurt it upon them."

Exultantly they began their preparations. Puukonhoya, the Little War God, donned his warbonnet with warrior feathers tied to the top that distinguished him from all others. On his back he hung his quiver of mountain lion skin, and, besides his bow and arrow, fletched with the wing of a bluebird, he carried his lightning. Palunhoya wore no bonnet, but only warrior feathers, while across his left shoulder he wore a bandoleer. In addition to his bow and arrow, he carried that ancient weapon, an egg-shaped stone tied with a piece of finely dressed buckskin to the end of a stick. Such a fine sight they were that their grandmother's eyes gleamed with pride.

With singing hearts they started out upon their perilous journey, thinking nothing of danger or hardship so that they might reach the presence of the mighty Tawa. Over desert and torrent, over mountain and valley, they journeyed tirelessly, fast and far, until at last they reached the Great Sky Canyon, far to the sunrise. Beyond them, Great Bear, Mountain Lion, and the venomous Gatoya, Guardian of All Angry Snakes, keeping their sleepless watch, and beyond them Closing Canyon barred the way.

First they came to a trail which led to these fierce watchers. It lay along a narrow ledge between the bare face of a vertical cliff and a steep precipice whose jagged depths sank sheer to the Underworld. It was in the narrowest part of this dangerous trail that they came upon an old, old man who sat with his back against the face of the cliff and his skinny knees drawn high against his wrinkled chin. So seamed and brown was his body that he might well have passed unnoticed until too late by eyes less vigilant than those of the Twins, for verily he looked a part of the rock himself. Inert and harmless, too, as the rocky wall he looked, but when the Twins would have made their way past him, with lightning quickness and venom, his lean, shrivelled legs shot out in a savage attempt to knock the beloved twain into the depths of the cruel precipice.

Not so easily, though, were the Twins to be caught napping. Just in time they leapt back and saved themselves from being hurtled into those cavernous depths.

"What do you mean by doing that way, Old One," roared Puukonhoya. "We have not done anything to you."

With false humility the Old One bent his sly face and whined protestingly: "Alas, there is no place in the world for the aged. Sitting on this narrow ledge, my old legs got cramped, and I but stretched them out a bit to relieve the cramp. I meant no harm to such fine lads as you two."

But the wise Twins knew that he spoke with a

double tongue and determined to give him no second chance; besides, they were eager to try the magic of the charm bestowed upon them by their grandmother. So the Youth chewed a bit of the meal and spurted it upon the treacherous, withered legs. Mighty Spider Woman! The magic nahu worked instantly, and the troublesome legs of the malignant old one drew up to his chin with a creaking of ancient joints, and were held there fast until the two had safely passed him.

Not far were they allowed to proceed unmolested, however, and suddenly, without warning, a thick gray shape reared up from the gloom, while a hideous head shot forth a stream of poison that would have meant speedy death to the bold adventurers. Again they leapt lithely back from this new danger, and before the enemy could make a fresh onslaught the magic flour was spurted on him. The venomous Gatoya was pacified the moment the nahu touched him, and the Twins marched on in triumph.

Brave and alert, the two pressed onward, their eyes keen to spy out danger, their flexible muscles ready for instant action. They had need to be so prepared for only a short distance, for two angry bears with glaring eyes sprang forward to crush them in their hairy embraces. Not thus, however, were the beloved twain to die— another leap and they were again out of danger —another spurt of the magic meal and the growling ones had become meek and quiet.

Fierce snarls proceeding from lip-bared teeth gave the only warning of their next menace, and had not Puukonhoya had ready on his tongue the never failing charm it had gone ill with them. Long sinewy bodies, capable of far greater leaps than any the Twins were capable of, came at them so that no backward leap could have saved them in this emergency. But the nahu met these lithe bodies in midair, and they sank with a soft thud to the ground and remained passive. There remained now only Closing Canyon for them to pass — but what a barrier!

The sky is solid at this point, and the walls constantly open and close like giant jaws ready to catch and crush any rash person attempting to pass the forbidden portals. The Twins stood and watched them ruefully and soon saw that, even though with extreme agility one might manage to leap through, the second could not fail to be caught in the crushing walls. As there seemed nothing else to do, Puukonhoya determined to try the effect of the nahu on the oscillating sky. Both of the Twins, therefore, spurted the nahu on the walls at the same time, and as the medicine spread itself over their sides the walls hung motionless for the moment it was necessary for the graceful bodies of the Twins to dart through.

At last they arrived at the beautiful turquoise kiva of their father and their mother. Huzrui-wuhti was overjoyed to see them. Her mother heart spied out their weariness, and she laid out their tired young bodies on mats of sweet grass. It seemed to them, tired as they were, that they had hardly fallen asleep when they were awakened by a most terrific crash upon the roof-top above them. Instantly they beheld their mighty father descending the pearl-encrusted ladder in his gleaming buckskins. It was easy to see that the Sun God was in a great rage, for his eyes sparkled angrily and he hung up his burnished shield so roughly that it clanged out a fierce war cry. His glowing splendor, heightened by his wrath, made him terrible to look upon.

"I smell strange children here," he thundered. "When men go away do their wives receive the embraces of strangers. Alas, for thy faith, Huzruiwuhti, bring forth these strange children whom you have."

With a smile Huzruiwuhti confidently led forth the Twins, but Tawa refused to listen to her. Instead of recognizing his sons, he looked at them without pity for their comeliness, and fiercely dragged them to the far end of his kiva. There stood a huge flint oven, and into this their father, whom they had dared so much to see, thrust them angrily. Then, still refusing to listen to the tearful mother, he built a raging fire. Alas! Kokyanwuhti, did you prepare your beloved grandsons against every danger save that of the jealous wrath of their own father.

The fire raged along with the anger of Tawa, at white heat for a long time, until at last both burned themselves out, and the Sun God arose and opened the great door so as to remove the charred bodies he expected to find within. Marvel of marvels! He started back and, quite unharmed, the Twins leaped out, laughing and dancing about his great knees. Not so easily could the Twins be destroyed, for Spider Woman had watched over her own. A radiant smile, brilliant as sunrise, swept over the anger-torn features of Tawa. He knew that of all created beings none but his own sons could have endured this fiery test, and so he gathered them to him and acknowledged them as his own sons.

Puukonhoya Wins a Bride

THERE ONCE LIVED, in one of the Oraibi villages, a very pretty maiden. The butterfly whorls of her black hair were larger and more lustrous than those of any other maids in the neighborhood, and her soft, brown eyes were full of the magic that made all of the young men wish to have her for their own. But the maiden would not have anything to do with any of them, nor did her family make any advances toward marriage with any of their families. The celebrated Twins, Puukonhoya and Palunhoya, heard about this matter, and it piqued their interest. When they had seen her, it was all over with them, for they found her so desirable that nothing would do but that they, too, woo her to see if they might succeed where all others had failed. But the more they thought of all the others who had failed, the more determined were they that they must not do likewise; so they thought they had better get the great Spider Woman to help them.

"Grandmother," they said to her, "there is a very strange thing over there in the village. A very pretty maiden lives there—we have seen her—and she will not have anything to do with any of the young men. It is very sad. We are going to see if we cannot do something about it. We are going to try too."

"Ha, you poor little ones. What makes you so proud as to think so rare a one will look at you when so many others have failed?"

"Yes, but we are going to try," they insisted even though her words made them somewhat crestfallen.

"That is all right, go on and try. But I tell you, so beautiful a one will never look at creatures so small and ugly," and this she said because the Twins had had so much praise and adulation she was afraid that they were getting to think too highly of themselves.

They had thought and talked to each other a great deal about the matter, so that very evening they set off for the village with some very fine squash seeds in their pouches. Now, not far from Oraibi, there were great quantities of mice living among the rocks. Stopping there, they gathered some sticks and set up a number of stone traps which they baited with the squash seeds. They had chosen a place in full view of the maiden's house, and they had made themselves fine in all their bravest attire. The maiden was not long in spying out these strange, fine-looking young men, and so she walked over that way to see about it.

"What are you two doing so busily that you do not see people?" she inquired sweetly.

"Yes," they replied, "we are setting traps for mice."

"Oh, but you should see the mice at our house—there are numbers and numbers. You come over to my house and set your traps there."

This was just the way they had planned it, so they followed her gladly and when they arrived at her mother's house fell to work setting traps every place that the maiden told them to and taking as long as possible in order to keep her with them. When they came to the mealing bins they asked her mother for a piki bread tray, and when she had brought it they used that, instead of a stone, to set the trap with.

"Now, tomorrow you look after the traps. It will go better that way," they cautioned the maiden.

Leaving there, they set out immediately to hunt an antelope, and when they spied one they killed it with their magic lightning so that it would show no wound. Then, when night had fallen, they secretly stole into the maiden's house and stealthily placed the great carcass under the piki bread tray so it would look as though their trap had caught it. This would make the maiden think they were something very much!

The maiden had been so impressed with the strange young men that she could hardly wait for morning to come so that she could go the rounds of the traps as she had been told to do. Imagine her astonishment when she came to the mealing bin and found, not a mouse, but great horns sticking out from under the tray! It had never been like this before.

"Come, my father," she screamed excitedly. "You go in there and be very quick about it. Something very large has been caught in the trap of the strange young men."

He was still sleeping when she called, and he rubbed his eyes when he came upon the strange sight, thinking he must be still in a dream.

"Thanks, thanks," he gasped in wonder. "Why, this is an antelope! Surely this is magic, for truly an antelope has been caught in the piki bread tray trap."

He lost no time in carrying the great carcass into the kiva to dress it and cut it up. The fine hide was saved for clothing, part of the meat was cooked for dinner and yet there was a lot left for drying, and the whole family was filled with joy and gratitude.

In the evening the Twins again took squash seeds and began to set traps near the maiden's house, just as they had before. She had been so sought after that they had decided to act just as if they had forgotten that they had ever met her. Having feasted on the antelope, the maiden was feeling very pleasant, and, furthermore, she had found these fine young men who did not seek her out very interesting. So she lost no time in strolling over to where the two were busily setting their traps.

"So, you have come again," she said smiling. "If you feel that way, come over to our house

[65]

again and set your traps there. Such mouse trapping we have never seen. Surely you must be some great ones, for something large was caught there last night under the piki bread tray, and we are all very happy about it."

They were only too glad to go with her and set busily to work making traps all over the house again. They were fixing the piki tray trap again when the father came over to watch them.

"Ha, you are setting that trap again?"

"That is it," they answered.

"That is well," he replied. "Last night an antelope was caught in this trap here; we have eaten of it and are very happy about it. You two are very clever; you have put an end to something here. That daughter of mine has been very haughty; she would have nothing to do with getting married. That seems to be changing now, so if anything is caught in this again come back in the evening and get the girl."

This time the Twins set off to find a deer, and when they had secured one they again entered the maiden's house by stealth and placed the game under the piki tray trap. Again, the maid found horns sticking out from under the tray when she visited it in the morning.

"My father, come quickly, it is the same again," she cried in great excitement. "There is again something large and horned in the trap."

"Thanks, thanks," said the delighted father. "Now this time it is a deer we have. Those two might even be the beloved Twins." Carrying it to the kiva as before, he dressed it and cut it up even as he had done the antelope. Again, part of it was eaten but the greater part was prepared for drying, and there was now a great quantity of fine meat outside the house.

"Tonight you had better wait for somebody here," said the father, smiling knowingly at his daughter.

When evening came at the house of Spider Woman, the Twins began to get ready to go to the house of the mana when a bitter quarrel arose.

"We cannot both marry this mana—I am the one who should have her," Puukonhoya said to his brother.

"No, I am the one," insisted Palulkon.

They had almost come to blows when Spider Woman intervened, "Now why will you quarrel about this?" Spider Woman chided. "There is always another deer in the woods. Of course Puukonhoya shall have this maiden, for he is the older."

So Puukonhoya, with all the bright feathers on his warbonnet dancing gaily, went triumphantly to the maiden's house and found her in an upper chamber industriously grinding corn. A sudden shyness made him say, "I have come because your father wanted it that way."

"That is all right. I will call my father," smiled the mana.

So the father came to Puukonhoya and said, "Yes, I remember I told you you might have my daughter because of the big game you caught for us and which we have been eating. It made us all very happy."

Then, after the mother had filled a tray with the meal the maiden had ground according to Hopi custom, Puukonhoya led her away to his grandmother's house to marry her. Spider Woman was greatly pleased about all this; she welcomed them both warmly and took the tray of meal from the girl. Returning, she set before her a small quantity of cornmeal pudding and bade her eat. There was so little, however, that the mana put it all into her mouth at once.

"Oh," cried the Spider Woman, "you must not eat it that way. Why, that is very something. Take just a bit of it in your mouth at one time and then see what you will see."

So the maid returned the food to the tray, and she found that when she put only a small bite in her mouth it increased until her mouth was filled. When her hunger was fully satisfied there still remained food on the tray.

That night the maid slept in Spider Woman's bed beside her, and in the morning they went out very early to throw prayer meal to the sun. When they returned Spider Woman shelled some corn and gave it to the mana, and she was busy three days at the grinding stone. On the fourth day, at yellow dawn, the Spider Woman went out and invited in all the neighbors to be present at the head-washing of the bride and groom. Then she led forth the maiden and told her to sit close to the kiva entrance and wait. Hardly had she done so than, in the strangest manner, threatening black clouds began to gather overhead, and presently great rain drops fell on the maiden, washing and bathing her.

Spider Woman now lifted her face to the clouds and said, "Thanks, that you have washed the bride. You may go now."

Again the maiden was set to the backbreaking labor of grinding corn, as all Hopi brides must do, and in the evening she prepared food from it. Spider Woman also added food that she brought from an inner chamber, and all the wedding party feasted. The next day this was repeated, and she made some tamales, and in this way, day after day, the little maiden prepared food for them all. But, instead of the shrill happy songs that the Hopi brides always sing, none came from her lips. Her heart was sad and her lips mute, for she was thinking, "Why do I not see the menfolk carding and spinning cotton for my wedding garment as the menfolk always do?"

It was true. Instead of making his bride's wedding finery, Puukonhoya and his brother did nothing all day but play with ball and stick or shoot their feathered arrows. Her heart was so sad that she took no note of how Spider Woman passed her frequently to go into an inner chamber nor did she hear her murmur, "That is going nicely, thanks, thanks," to someone within.

Finally Spider Woman came to the maiden and said, "You must prepare some cornmeal and wheat pudding now, for I am going to send you back to your parents. They are homesick for you."

The poor girl's heart sank still lower, but she unquestioningly made cornmeal pudding as she had been bidden. But in the morning she found that Spider Woman had prepared the yucca suds

[69]

in which to wash her head and Puukonhoya's. Then she saw Spider Woman come from the inner chamber with her arms heaped high with the most beautiful bridal costume she had ever seen, and her face beamed with happiness again. All the time that she had been worrying spiders had been busily spinning on her blanket and girdle, and they could not have been more beautifully done. After Spider Woman had dressed her in these garments, she brought out a great quantity of meat and gave it to her grandson, saying as she bade them farewell, "Now, Puukonhoya, I must caution you to act right when you go to your bride's home. Do not talk too much, for it is not proper for a young man to do so. You sit with your arms folded over your knees looking modestly at your wristbands. Thus does a proper Hopi groom behave himself."

The two then set out for the maiden's home, Puukonhoya carrying the meat on his back and both of them very happy thinking about their new life together. From a housetop watchers saw them coming and called out "Hao, someone is coming," so all were out to welcome them to her mother's house. A great feast was prepared from the meat that Puukonhoya had brought, and after it had all been eaten all sat about and talked or sang songs. That is, all but Puukonhoya talked. He refused to say a single word but sat on the floor with his arms folded across his knees. That would have been all right, but instead of looking down modestly at his wristband he took it off and holding it before his eyes stared out through it at the assembled company.

The people did not know what to make of so strange a proceeding. They said among themselves, "So that is his custom is it. That is the way he does. To be sure, we have never seen it so, but what of that?" But still they felt uncomfortable, and Puukonhoya could see that everything was not as it should be.

Early the next morning, Puukonhoya raced all the way back to his grandmother's to tell her how things had gone. She immediately asked him if he had done as she told him to about the wristlet.

"Oh, yes," he replied confidently, "When the feast was over and the talk started I would not answer anyone. I just took off my wristband and looked at them through it. I could tell that they thought I was very something."

"Very something, indeed! I should think they would have, you great stupid one," groaned Spider Woman. "It is not done as you did it. When one becomes a son-in-law he is supposed to sit there with his arms folded upon his knees and close before his face so that he appears to be looking at his arm bands—not through them! You are ka (not) hopi."

Puukonhoya was sorry about this, although it did not worry him very much and he thought his grandmother had made altogether too much fuss about it. But he returned to his father-in-law determined to be a model bridegroom. Soon after, the men began to plant, so he returned to his grandmother and said, "It is planting time now and we are going to plant. Have you anything to do about this, so that I shall look very something?"

"Very well," she said, "you take this and plant it, and be sure you plant no other."

When the father-in-law saw the tiny ear she had given him, he said, "That is a very small amount for planting. That will not be enough."

"Yes, let us use mine," insisted Puukonhoya. "You will find that it is a great deal to plant before we finish."

His father-in-law thought the new groom must be a very lazy person. But he yielded to him, and they took only the small ear into the field to plant. Now Puukonhoya put only one grain into the hole he made with his planting stick, and when he saw his father-in-law putting a great many seeds in the first hill, as all Hopi do, he stopped him.

"That is not the way to do it. Put only one grain to each hill. That will be plenty."

The father-in-law did not believe him, but thought as it was Puukonhoya's field he would do as he wished. When the entire field had been planted, he could hardly believe his eyes when he saw that there was still seed in the small bag from which they were planting. It was magic corn and had kept on increasing. When the rains came and the corn burst through, it was so lusty and green that there had never been seen such fine plants before. In course of time, however,

[72]

much grass appeared in the field with the corn and threatened to choke it. Now, as Puukonhoya had never done any field work before, he did not know what to do about this, so he again sought his grandmother for advice.

"Have you planted?" she asked.

"It is so," he answered.

"And when it rained did the grass and weeds come up to choke the corn?"

"It was just that way," he replied sadly.

"A son-in-law is supposed to help his father-in-law take care of his field, so you return and do that. Take a hoe and form little ant hills all through the field," said Spider Woman, referring to the small furrows of earth that a hoe makes when the field is worked.

"That is fine," said Puukonhoya cheerfully. "I will do it just as you say."

Returning to his wife's home, he asked for a hoe and hurried right off to the field with it, so anxious was he to do the right thing. Here he laid aside the hoe and went all about the field looking for something. Finally, he stopped because he had found a fine large ant hill. He then carefully gathered up into his blanket both ants and ant hill. Then what a time he had, going up and down the rows of corn making small ant hills out of the great one he had found. It was tiresome work, and when it was done he was so pleased with his industry that he rushed right off to his grandmother to tell her about it.

"I told you to hoe the corn yesterday. Now I hope you have done it. And how much did you hoe?"

"Yes, you told me the way yesterday, so I went right back to the field and hunted until I had found an ant hill that was just right. Such an ant hill as it was! The very grandfather of all ant hills. I took it all up in my blanket, and it took me all afternoon to make small ones all through the corn as you told me to. It was very hard to do, but I do not mind if you are pleased."

"Now, that is the way you have done again," stormed the Spider Woman. "You certainly are a great fool. Please — I told you to do quite a different thing that anyone should know. I meant by ant hills those ridges one makes when he cuts down the weeds with his hoe and draws the earth up around the base of the corn stalks. That is what I told you to do, dumbest one! You go back now and work the ground so that the dry crust will be broken up fine and the weeds turned under. You understand? I mean wiklolantanangwu."

Now Puukonhoya had been watching a bird fly overhead, so he only heard the last, "Yes, I understand, I will remember and do it right this time, wiklolantanangwu."

The next morning Puukonhoya asked his wife's mother for a little grease or fat. They hunted it up and gave it to him wondering what he wanted it for. Taking his hoe and the fat he went out to the field, but upon arriving there he laid aside his hoe. He then went busily up and down the field carefully scattering the fat along the rows, for this act is also expressed by the word "wiklolantanangwu." Then he took up his hoe and returned home.

[74]

He was sure he had succeeded in pleasing his grandmother this time so he visited her very early.

"So you have come again?" she asked.

"Yes," he replied.

"You remember what I told you yesterday, and have you done it right this time?"

"Oh, yes," he said happily, "I remembered what you said, wiklolantanangwu. So when we had eaten the morning meal I got some tallow from my wife's mother. Then I took it to the field and carefully put it all up and down the rows. Very right I did it."

"Alas, you are a fool—a very great fool," wailed the Spider Woman distractedly. "I told you to hoe the field, and you ought to know that it means to chop off the weeds and turn over the dry ground. This is the wiklolantanangwu I meant. Not the other. What good would the scattering of fat do to the weeds, may I ask you? Now you go and hoe that field as it should be done."

When Puukonhoya returned this time he found his father-in-law sitting thinking and looking very sad. He knew that Puukonhoya had been going to the field daily, but though he had gone there several times he could see no signs of any work having been done there. The grass was growing higher and higher, while the corn that once had looked so fine was dwindling. He began to feel that his daughter had got a good-for-nothing for a husband and wondered if he had better not send him back to his grandmother. It was while he was thus thinking that

Puukonhoya returned and, seeing his father-in-law so downcast, he asked him about it.

"Yes," said the man dejectedly, "I have been thinking about our field over there. The grass and weeds are doing fine, but the corn that was once so very fine is getting very tired. By this time the ears should be forming but instead of that the plants are drying up."

"So that is what you have been thinking about," said Puukonhoya cheerfully. "Now, you must not think that way any more. I know what to do now, so we will go there now and hoe the corn." So the two started off for the field.

But Spider Woman was so chagrined at the poor showing her grandson had made that she determined to take no more chances. Calling some clouds, she bade them go and hoe the field for Puukonhoya. So the two men had hardly got started with their hoeing of the hard ground when a cloud formed over the San Francisco Mountains. Soon many clouds were moving toward the village, and soon the rain was descending in such torrents that the two men were obliged to stop and run for shelter. The rain beat so fiercely on the ground that the water ran in little rivulets through the rows of corn covering up the weeds and grass with wet sand and earth. When the two returned after the rain, it was found that the corn had not been hurt but the weeds and grass had disappeared.

"Thanks, kind clouds, that you have cleaned up the field for us," said the old man gratefully. "We can go home now."

[76]

The corn sprang up as if by magic, and the ears formed almost overnight. From that time they began to live happily, for the heart of Puukonhoya was kind even though he was heedless, and he made up his mind to try to do better in the future.

The Youth Conquers Man-Eagle

WHENEVER THE GIGANTIC SHADOW of the terrible Man-Eagle appeared like a threatening cloud in the vast Above, young and old in a wild panic sought shelter. But no matter how swift their flight, always after one of his sudden raids and as sudden disappearances, when the people would gain sufficient courage to creep forth, it would be found that some beautiful maid or comely young wife had disappeared. And though his ravages affected the entire country, he went unpunished, for there seemed no one among all the Peaceful People valiant enough to attack him. And so for many years he continued his wicked raids, but at last he crossed the path of Puukonhoya, grandson of Spider Woman, the Mighty.

This was during the September moon at Old Walpi, when the Hopi women were celebrating the Lalakonti, or Basket Dance, with sacred plaques of their own weaving. The ninth morning of the ceremonies had arrived, and Tawa had graciously made the day bright and clear. On the trail over which the runners were to come stood a woman gorgeously arrayed. Her headbands supported symbolic rain clouds and to these were attached a horn and symbols of the squash blossom. Eagle tail feathers rose in clusters over her flowing black hair and were also attached to the half corncobs she held in each hand. Her slim young body was draped in a snowy blanket elaborately bordered in green and black, hung at the corners with heavy black tassels. It was Lakone Mana, the beloved wife of Puukonhoya.

As the day grew brighter tiny specks appeared far up the rocky trail. They grew larger with amazing rapidity, and amid the wildest tumult and excitement one figure drew far ahead of the rest and broke through the circle of priestesses on the dance plaza—Puukonhoya, of course, for none were so fleet as this magic Twin of Tawa. The sun rose higher, and at last came the priestesses to circle round the plaza singing in chorus, each with her basket plaque. With both hands the baskets were held bottom side out. And as the song continued, the bodies of the women swayed rhythmically, the baskets were raised first to one breast, then to the other and finally brought downward in a line with their hips. Next into this circle came two maids in ceremonial blankets and with bundles on their shoulders. All eyes centered on them as they untied the bundles and each held aloft a basket. Suddenly they threw their baskets high in the air so that they would fall in the midst of an eager crowd of young men.

What a melee followed—the wildest struggle

in which each wrestled in a determined effort to obtain a basket that would proclaim one of the winners in the contest. Excitement was at white heat as all eyes fastened on that squirming, struggling mass of menfolk. There were none to espy a sudden black blotch that marked itself ominously against the cloudless blue of the Above. Closer and closer, quite unnoticed, the black blotch descended. Then a sudden shrill scream of hurt and terror froze the romping warm blood of the merrymakers. Panic-stricken eyes turned upward toward the sound of those piercing screams which grew so rapidly fainter as the black blotch grew smaller against the sky from which it had so recently descended. "Kwataka, Man-Eagle," gasped terror-frozen lips. As they gazed, something small and birdlike fluttered down to fall among them—it was a half corn cob to which were attached eagle tail feathers.

"Lakone Mana, Lakone Mana," cried a youth's voice in hoarse agony, and "Lakone Mana" echoed more shrilly from many throats. It was true. Lakone Mana, in all her fresh young comeliness, was missing from among them. Then the Youth, Puukonhoya, arose terrible in his grief and anger vowing to rescue his bride and slay the monster who had too long ravaged the countryside unpunished.

Alone he set forth. Eager to come upon his foe he journeyed tirelessly and fiercely until he reached the foot of the San Francisco Mountains from whose towering summits he hoped to gain access to the sky in which was hidden the house of Man-Eagle. Just as he began his toilsome ascent he came upon two strange maidens dressed in mantles of pinyon bark and grass and, to his joy, not far from them sat Spider Woman with Mole beside her.

"So you have come," said his grandmother as he approached her. "Now where do you go so rapidly and what has happened that you look so sad?"

"Yes," groaned the wretched Puukonhoya, "that villain Kwataka has carried off my beautiful Lakone Mana, and I shall neither rest nor break my fast until I have taken her from him."

"Sit you down," ordered Spider Woman peremptorily. Then more kindly, "I will aid you." She beckoned to the two maidens who obediently drew closer. "These are the Pinyon Maids," she explained, and to them, "You go and gather pinyon gum, wash it and from it make something just like that flint arrowhead garment that Kwataka wears over his great wicked body."

So the maids bathed themselves for purification, gathered and washed the pinyon gum and with clever fingers made so exact an imitation of the fabulous flint armor that the sharpest eye could not detect any difference.

When it was completed Spider Woman, after examining the garment carefully, handed it to the Youth together with some magic charm meal; but hardly had he received it when he found that Spider Woman had disappeared. "Kokyan-wuhti, where have you gone?" he called loudly.

"Here on your right ear, stupid," she chuckled softly, and when Puukonhoya put his hand up quickly, sure enough, he found there a spider so tiny as to be invisible. "I will remain here unseen," she said, "so as to whisper advice in your ear when you most need it."

Then they left the Pinyon Maids, and Mole went before to show them the best way up the mountain's rugged sides to the topmost peak. Alas! even from here the sky was far, far above them. Just as the heart of the Youth began to sink with discouragement, Eagle came down with a swift swoop and stood beside them. With no delay they were on his back, and he soared aloft with them until he was so tired he could go no farther. Just then Hawk sailed so close that they were able to scramble onto his back, and his strong wings carried them yet higher into the air. Finally he too grew weary, and at that moment Gray Hawk relieved him and carried them farther into the Above. When he had reached the limit of his endurance Red Hawk, Palakwayo, drew near and received them. Up, up, up he beat his way with mighty pinions until, after flying an immense distance, they came at last to a passage in the sky at which Red Hawk stopped.

Through this, Puukonhoya, Spider Woman and Mole made their way. In the distance they could see, high on a bluff, the great white house where Man-Eagle lived and kept his victims. So eager was the Youth to meet the monster that he rushed forward to climb a huge ladder which offered the one means of approach to the house above.

[82]

"Stop foolish boy," commanded Spider Woman. "You cannot do it that way. You must know that each rung of that ladder is made of a stone with an edge so sharp that the hands and feet of anyone attemping to mount it would be cut to shreds. I know the way to fix that though. You pick a handful of sumac berries and give them to Lizard to chew. Then you will see something."

Obediently Puukonhoya did as she directed, and when he had returned with the berries he saw Lizard sliding out from a crack in the rocks to await him. After chewing the berries into a cud, Lizard handed it to the impatient Youth.

"Rub that on the sharp edges as you mount," cautioned Spider Woman. So Puukonhoya rubbed the sumac berry cud upon the knife-sharp edges, and they became so dull that he could mount without harm to his hands or feet. Stealthily the Youth crept along until he made his way into the stronghold of Man-Eagle. One of the first things he came upon was the great flint arrowhead armor hanging in an outer recess.

"Take it from its peg and in its place hang the one made by the Pinyon Maids," whispered Spider Woman. Quickly he did so, hiding the removed armor under his blanket. Then his heart boiled over in hot anger for he beheld in an inner recess his bride—with the great ugly head of Man-Eagle in her lap.

Without a heed of danger he called out lustily, "I have come, beloved. Fear not, I will soon have you again."

Great joy lit up the face of the captive little

bride, but it faded quickly into terror as she called, "No, no, Puukonhoya, you cannot do anything, for no one ever leaves this terrible place alive. Fly and save yourself while there is yet time."

But Puukonhoya replied, "Not so, have no fear for me. You will soon be in my arms."

Now it had fared ill with Puukonhoya had not Spider Woman sprinkled forth some of the magic meal such as she had given the Youth, and this deadened the ears of Man-Eagle. But even so, as if feeling a strange presence, he awakened and strode out to put on his armor so as to start out on another of his cruel raids. Without the least suspicion he took the counterfeit armor and put it on. But, as he started out, he discovered the Youth in the entrance and with a shriek of rage demanded of him what he wanted.

"I have come to take my bride away from you," said the Youth bravely.

Amused at the bravado of the small stripling, Man-Eagle thought it would be amusing to play with this new prey before killing him, so he responded genially, "Aha, my young turkey-cock, we will have to gamble to decide that. You will have to abide by the consequences though, for if you lose, as you surely will, I will kill you and keep the pretty bride for my own embraces."

"It is well," boasted Puukonhoya. "Let it be that way, I will not fail."

Man-Eagle grinned horribly and brought forth a pipe larger than the head of Puukonhoya. Filling it with bitter, black tobacco, he handed it to the stripling. "You must smoke this entirely out," he said, "and if you become dizzy or sick in your stomach you fail."

Puukonhoya took the huge pipe and inhaled deeply while the monster watched him with a smile of cruel confidence. The Youth not only kept the pipe aglow, but though he exhaled no smoke he seemed to feel no ill effect. Man-Eagle was filled with amazement, for how could he know that the smoke was passing through Puukonhoya's body into an underground passage that Mole had dug for it.

"Ho, stripling," he said in great wrath, "what trick is this? What have you done with all that smoke?"

Spider Woman whispered, and Puukonhoya for answer led him to the door. Waving the great pipe toward where dense clouds of black smoke were issuing from each of the Four World Quarters, he smiled, and Man-Eagle knew he had lost that bout. But now, Kwataka set the hero a second test by bringing forth two huge deer antlers, saying, "We will now each choose one of these, and he who fails to break the antler he chooses is beaten," and he lay one antler to the northwest while the other he placed to the southeast.

Spider Woman whispered to the Youth to demand first choice, but this Man-Eagle refused. Four times Puukonhoya demanded this, taunting Kwataka with cowardice, and at last Man-Eagle yielded. While they had been arguing, the tiny spider had crept unobserved to examine and found that the antler at the northwest was a real

[85]

antler, while the one on the southeast was only a clever imitation of brittle wood though it looked much the heavier. Puukonhoya was much surprised when Spider Woman told him to choose the heavier pair, but he obeyed and was therefore able to break apart the prongs of the brittle antler with but small effort while in vain did Man-Eagle strive with the real one. He could not make even the tiniest fracture appear in the polished horn surface. So a second time was Kwataka defeated.

"This is to be your next trial," quoth Man-Eagle, leading Puukonhoya to where two large pine trees grew tall and strong, close to the house. "You choose one of the trees, I will take the other, and whoever plucks up one by the roots will win." Now Spider Woman, who knows all, had been able to foresee this test and had sent Mole to burrow under one of the trees and gnaw off all the roots. When he had done this he came quickly back through the tunnel, emerging spotless, even to his pink nose, and sat there spotless to await the outcome of the contest.

Softly Spider Woman whispered to Puukonhoya, "Choose the tree by which your Uncle Mole is sitting." So Puukonhoya strode confidently to that tree and, encircling it with muscular young arms, plucked it easily from the ground and tossed it over the edge of the cliff. Man-Eagle was dumbfounded. Feeling sure that Puukonhoya would fail in this test, he had not expected to have his own strength brought to trial, but there was no way out. He struggled mightily with the standing tree but was unable to uproot that which had long withstood the mighty winds of the Four World Quarters and was obliged to admit defeat again.

Almost at his wits' end for further tests for this remarkable young man, Man-Eagle next had an enormous amount of food spread out on the floor and told Puukonhoya that he must eat it all at one sitting. Here was a task. Yet the Youth did not hesitate. One food basin after another was emptied—meat, bread and porridge magically disappeared. When the last basin was emptied and there remained not even a crumb, the Youth showed no sign of being satisfied.

"What, have you nothing more for me to eat? I am very hungry," he complained. Again Uncle Mole had come to his rescue by digging a deep hole beside him to receive the food, and Puukonhoya was able to come forth victor for the fourth time.

Man-Eagle was really desperate as he prepared the fifth test. Making a huge pile of pine faggots, he directed Puukonhoya to seat himself upon it. "I shall now set fire to this, and we will see how you are able to endure the flames. If you come forth unharmed I will take the same test," he said smiling evilly. Quite undaunted, the young man took his seat atop the wood pile, because underneath his tunic he wore the real flint arrowhead garment. Man-Eagle eagerly applied the flaming brand to the huge wood pile at the Four Cardinal Points, and at once fierce flames licked out hungrily at Puukonhoya like fierce wolves. But the arrowheads of the armor were coated with ice, which began to melt so that the water trickled down and kept the Youth from catching fire. When the pile had been entirely consumed there sat Puukonhoya absolutely unharmed and smiling pleasantly.

The monster's amazement knew no bounds, and his grief equalled his wonder when he saw Puukonhoya begin to gather wood for his test. But, still thinking he had on his own flint arrowhead garment, he seated himself without any alarm. The Youth in turn ignited the fire just as his opponent had done, and again the flames leapt hungrily toward their prey. But this time it was different, for when they sprang at Kwataka the flames bit greedily at the imitation gum garment. With a roar it burst into flames and in a wink Man-Eagle had disappeared.

"You have won," said Spider Woman, "and so you can afford to be generous," whispered Spider Woman to her grandson. "Now you approach the fire and spurt some of the meal I gave you upon it."

Hardly had the meal fallen on the glowing embers than a handsome man arose from them. In a stern voice Spider Woman now addressed him. "Will you stop killing people and carrying off our maidens? Will you forsake your evil ways and make your heart good?"

"I will do all you ask, Kokyanwuhti," said Kwataka humbly.

Puukonhoya had been unable to restrain his eagerness to seek out his wife while this was

[88]

going on. He ran to the house to find her cowering in a dark corner as she awaited the outcome of the tests between her young husband and the terrible Man-Eagle. Imagine her joy when, instead of the monster, her own Puukonhoya returned and clasped her to him. Hand in hand they ran to all the other chambers in the great white house and released all the other captive women who had been stolen from the Peaceful People and other tribes, for there were many in the monster's lair.

Red Hawk now flew down on the cliff and awaited them. It took but a moment for the Youth, Spider Woman and Mole to get on his back, and in his arms Puukonhoya held tightly his beloved Lakone Mana. With a mighty stirring of wings Red Hawk began the journey back, and they returned to their home in the same manner they had come.

The Youth and the Eagles

A YOUNG HOPI LAD THERE WAS named Chorzhvuki-quole which means Long-Bunch-of-Bluebird-Wing-Feathers. He lived with his parents and two sisters and was a fine enough lad in his way, but he did not help his old father with the field work as he should. Instead, he was always off on the cliffs hunting and catching eagles or getting food for those he had in his pen. When his angry sisters would scold him for not helping his father to earn their frugal living, he would only excuse himself by saying that he had to take care of his eagles. As soon as the warm weather started he would be about this business, but there came a spring when he was very sad because all of his penned eagles had been used for ceremonial purposes and he had been able to catch only two small new ones.

"What god have I offended that it should come about this way," he complained bitterly. "It never used to be this way. I, who have always had so many fine big eagles, have now only these two small ones." But he carried home the two small eagles and spent as much time upon them as he had on the numbers he had formerly possessed. His poor old father was left alone to struggle against the grass and weeds in the field morning after morning while the young man was out hunting food for his eagles. Finally the mother and sisters decided that they must help the old man since Chorzhvukiquole would not, but the girls were very angry about it. Already they had to spend long weary hours at the grinding stones grinding the meal, of which he ate no small amount, and it seemed most unfair that they should now have to shoulder his duties as well.

The more they thought about it the angrier they got, so one day they caught the eagles and beat them severely. Then, before returning with their mother to the field, they locked the door and hid the wooden key in the ashes of the outside fireplace. "Now maybe this will punish that worthless one who makes other people do his work. Maybe he will think some long thoughts when he finds that he cannot get in to drink from the heavy earthen jars we have carried on our heads from that faraway spring way down there."

Just as they thought, the youth returned later in the day very tired and thirsty. He could hardly wait to get to the big earthen jars and get a cool draft from them. He could not believe it when he found the door locked. "Well, how is this," he said, angrily shaking at the door. "Never in all my life has it been like this before. Someone has locked this door."

"Yes," screamed one of the eagles shrilly, "that is what those bad sisters of yours have done. They hid the key in some ashes over there in the fireplace."

Chorzhvukiquole stared in amazement to hear one of his eagles talking, but, sure enough, when he had poked about in the ashes there was the key so that he was able to get into the house and quench his thirst. He was very grateful to his eagle because his throat had been parched, and while he fed them they talked about the sisters.

"Those sisters of yours were very mean and angry," said the eagles. "Surely we had done them no harm and yet they beat us sorely. They locked the water away from you just because you were out looking for food for us. Very wicked girls!"

"They did it just they way you say," agreed the young man.

"You go and dress yourself up," suggested one of the eagles, "and we will give you a ride on our backs to the field where they are working. They will think you are very something when they see you flying above them. They have been very bad and it will make them very angry."

This seemed to be a good thing to do to Chorzhvukiquole, so he painted his legs bright yellow and tied many rattles upon them. He put on his best kilt and tied some eagle tail feathers in his hair. Then he painted his body different colors and tied on a bright sash. Across his cheeks and nose he painted a black band, hung pendants in his ears and many strings of bright beads about his neck. He was most splendid!

[92]

After praising him, one of the eagles said, "You get on my back and I will carry you. We will show those girls whether they should beat eagles and lock away the water from thirsty people."

How the heart of the boy leapt as he mounted the eagle's back! To think that he should now skim away through the air as he had so often watched the eagles do, lying there on his back at the cliff's edge. One eagle led the way upward, and the other flew so close that the youth held to it with both hands. The people of the village looked on this strange sight with wide eyes and recognizing the youth cried out, "Ah, that is what comes of hunting eagles all the time. One of them is now carrying off Chorzhvukiquole."

Four times they circled over the village before flying to the field where the family was at work. "Now you sing a song that will make your sisters look up and see who you are flying so fine and high while people are working," said one eagle. So, as they circled over the field, Chorzhvuki-quole's clear high voice sang this song:

Haoo Inguu! Haoo Inaa!	*Hao, my mother! Hao, my father!*
Itah uuyiyuu kamuktiqoo,	*Our corn grows high,*
Shilakwayata,	*Corn husks*
Tutubena, tutubena,	*Are figured, are figured,*
Ayay, tutubena,	*Aha, are figured,*
Tutubena, tutubena,	*Are figured, are figured,*
Yaaa!	*Yaaa!*

As the little song floated to them the maidens quickly raised their heads and rested on their hoes. The song was one they had sung when they were children and told how they used to fold the corn husks over and pierce them into designs with their sharp little teeth so that when they were unfolded and held to the light a pattern would appear. "Our brother is coming to help us at last," they cried, "because we can hear him singing."

They became quite bewildered when, though they could hear his song, they could not see him on the path. Then the eagles swooped very low and it was plain the song came from above. When they looked up and saw their brother on the eagle's back all their crossness vanished and their hearts sank in terror at his peril. "Oh, you wicked eagles," they cried wildly, "you are bad ones who made all the trouble, and now you are carrying away our brother!"

The eagles screamed a shrill cry of triumph and their feathers stood erect on their bodies, but they made no answer. The old parents stretched out their arms toward them and besought the birds to bring down their son, but the eagles only screamed again and beat their way up higher. Four times they circled these terror-stricken folk —four times the lad sang the foolish little song. The last notes floated down like an echo the eagles had gone so high, and in a moment more they had vanished entirely from the despairing eyes of the lad's family. Nay, Chorzhvukiquole, himself, began to be alarmed at the strange actions of the eagles, for until now he had thought it but a bit of fun and had expected to descend and allay the fears of his sisters after they had been frightened a bit.

"Now, why do you do it this way?" he cried as they continued to fly higher. "It was enough the way we have done it. Let us go down again." His only answer was another shrill scream from the eagles and a bristling of the feathers against his bare flesh. Higher and yet higher they flew —the highest cliff below was wiped out, and finally they passed through a hole in the sky. They were now in the land where the eagles live and from which they come in answer to Hopi prayers to hatch their eaglets. Far to the eastward could be seen a high bluff from which gleamed the many white houses of the eagles, and toward this spot the birds flew.

On a high and lonely crag of this bluff the eagles descended and bade the youth dismount, saying, "Here you can stay now because your sisters beat us and were bad to us."

"Now why should you act this way?" reproached the lad. "Have I not fed you and cared for you so that you have grown from weaklings into big fine birds? The eagles where you nest below have belonged to our tribe for many grandfathers back to a time very, very when, and none of them have ever done as you are now doing." But even as he reproached them the eagles rose in the air and deserted him.

After the youth had looked desperately on every side for a means of escape he saw that there was no way out for him. The sheer sides of the lofty pinnacle offered no slightest foothold for a great distance below. His heart almost failed him, and he wondered whether he had not better end it at once by leaping from the bluff.

"If I remain here I shall only die slowly after suffering the torments of thirst and starvation," he thought despairingly, "so why not be done with the matter and jump to the sharp rocks far below."

As if in answer to his desperate thought a tiny wren came hopping gaily along the cliff's edge. "Tell me, Brother Wren," he asked, "is there any way to get down from this bluff save by flying or jumping?" But the wren made him no answer and in a moment saddened him still further by flying away. He was again about to carry out his desperate purpose when the wren returned hopping along the cliff just as before. This time though, following behind it was a big, black spider.

"Now don't you think that way any more," said the spider as if reading his thought. "That wren told me about you. You poor one, you are all alone. Well, you just stay here." With those words the spider, too, left him, in spite of the pitying words, as if it had just come to taunt him and add to his misery. But in a few moments two turkey feathers seemed to be creeping slowly toward him, and from under them presently the spider crawled forth.

"You take these and keep yourself warm with them. You sleep on one and cover yourself with the other," the spider said. "It grows very cold up here at night. My heart is sad for you, my grandson. It is too bad that those eagles to whom you have been so good should have treated you so meanly."

Then without warning it disappeared, and

Chorzhvukiquole began to think how badly the eagles had treated him and how it had been better had he spent his time helping his family instead of on the ungrateful birds. When the bitter night air crept into his veins he bethought him of the turkey feathers, and though it seemed impossible that such small things could add to his warmth he determined to do as the spider had bid. Putting one feather on the ground, he lay on it and it spread itself out into a thick soft bed, and placing the other on his chest it grew into a big fleecy cover.

Early the next morning Wren again appeared. "So you are here again," said the youth more cheerful after his comfortable night's rest, but the wren did not reply. It hopped to the place on the bluff where the spider had come up and beckoned with its tiny head for the boy to follow. When he had moved cautiously over, he could see a narrow crevice that reached to the ground below, but it was too smooth to afford him the slightest foothold.

Wren now began to pull from its wings one feather after another and to fit them across the crack at short intervals, one below the other like the rungs of a ladder, holding herself to the sides of the crevice with her claws. When the feathers from the wings were all used, it pulled out the tail feathers, but when these were all used, it was still far to the bottom. So it began to pull out the small feathers from all over the body so as to complete the ladder. Still the bottom had not been reached, so the brave little creature pulled out the soft down that grows beneath the feathers and used that. When Wren returned up the magic ladder the poor little thing was quite naked, having stripped itself of everything but her bill. Now it spoke for the first time. "You follow me down the ladder. It will be all right; you need have no fear."

When they had made their way safely to the ground, Wren said, "Now you wait here until I come back." Returning to the ladder, it made its way back up the crack, pulling out feather by feather with its bill and replacing them in its own body. When the little creature had reached the top it was again clothed in all its feathers and flew back to the youth. "Now go and find the spider," it said and pointed out the way.

Thankfully Chorzhvukiquole set out and journeyed until he was stopped by a voice at his feet. "Step back a little," it cried. "You are almost on my house." He stepped quickly back and saw a spider hole at his feet. "Come in," the voice invited.

"How can that be, when the hole is so small?" he asked.

In the wink of an eye the spider appeared, and again as quickly it changed and Spider Woman herself stood before him. Removing the small sticks and grass around the opening, she made it possible for him to enter. "Now," she said kindly, "you must be very hungry. Those eagles you were so good to certainly have been very bad to you."

"Yes, I have been thinking about that," he said ruefully.

"Well, you had better be done with them and live with me now. I think you had better think a lot about the way you did for those eagles instead of helping your father with the field work. You will learn some things here and then you can go back to them and help them." Then she brought him a tiny piece of meat, a small bit of doughy mush and half a nut. He was so hungry that he felt he could eat at least a whole antelope, and he felt very sad about these small morsels.

"Alas! I am so famished what good will so small an amount do me? Surely I shall starve here too." But he determined to take what he could, and he put the mush into his mouth.

Spider Woman stopped him, "Oh, you do not do it that way. Take only a little bit on your tongue and see what then. As for the meat, you must just suck that." To his delight, when he did as she said the tiniest bit of mush expanded in his mouth until it was entirely filled. The same was true of the nut and the meat, so from the small quantity he made a good meal.

After he had eaten, Spider Woman made him a ball of pitch and hair, and in the morning he left the house kicking the ball before him in true Hopi fashion. He ran to the south after it and arrived at the shore of a small lake upon which were many little birds. For the first time he thought of someone else, and, remembering Spider Woman's kindness to him and her fondness for such game, he killed one of the birds for her. On his way back he kicked the ball before him and followed it. At the last kick it fell into the kiva so that Spider Woman knew he was coming.

"Thanks that you have come," she said gladly. "Now we will put this bird away that you have brought. We must not eat much of it at a time and it will last a long time."

Chorzhvukiquole laughed at her, "Yes, I will be nibbling at that great big bird a long time."

"But the meat I gave you first was from such a small bird that had been killed by a larger one, and I lived on that for some time."

But the youth determined to go out and get game for her the next day, and she thanked him warmly when he returned with more birds. "With such a hunter we will now be able to eat in the usual way instead of by magic. How ungrateful were those eagles for whom you found food." This was very pleasant of the youth, and it gave him a pleasant feeling to feel that he was returning her kindness to him.

The third day he took a throwing stick with him when he went to the small lake and so was able to bring back a great many little birds. Spider Woman said she did not know how she would get along without him when he returned to his parents, but she knew how glad they would be to have such a son to provide for them. And this made Chorzhvukiquole think how nice it would be to do this for his family who, he could now remember, had been so good to him when he had been very heedless. Then Spider Woman warned him that he must never travel to the west on his hunting trips because there was someone dangerous in that direction who might harm him.

On the fourth day he made a trip to the same lake, but the warning of Spider Woman had made him feel that he would like to know more about the danger that lay to the westward and what manner of person it was who was reported to be so bad. Instead of obeying Spider Woman, he felt that he could quickly run away if any danger threatened. So he kicked his ball to the westward and raced gaily after it. All at once the ball disappeared, and he found that it had dropped into a kiva; so he approached closer and stood there undecided what to do next.

"You have been seen, so come in; nobody will harm you," called out a voice from within.

So the youth went in and was received with so much kindness and invited so courteously to sit down and be comfortable that he could not believe that the one who lived there could be either dangerous or bad. But what a one was this man to look at! His eyelids were so long that they hung way down down over his chest and must be laid back whenever he wished to look at anything.

"I am Hasohkata," he told the young man. "What do you say to playing a little game—how about a game of chance?"

"It will be all right like that," said Chorzhvukiquole.

So they began to play, but though the youth did his best he soon had lost two games to Hasohkata. "What will you pay me now?" demanded the man in a harsh angry tone.

"I do not know," said Chorzhvukiquole,

[101]

startled by the man's changed manner. "I have nothing but my ball—you may have that."

"Pray, what should I want with that?" said Hasohkata scornfully. "Well then, if you have nothing to pay you can at least lie outside the entrance so as to keep the cold out for me."

It was fall weather and quite cold, but the lad agreed to pay his losses that way and started up the ladder. But Hasohkata said, "Oh, no, not so fast. I am afraid you will run away since you did not obey Spider Woman who was so good to you. I will just tie your hands and feet." So he did this, and the poor youth was not even able to kick his feet together or clap his hands to keep warm and soon grew wretchedly cold and miserable.

When Chorzhvukiquole did not return as usual, Spider Woman began to be uneasy and said to herself, "It is already half-noon and the lad is not here yet; undoubtedly he has not heeded my warning but has gone to the westward and fallen into the hands of bad people. That is the way these young things must do." So she started out to hunt for him and ere long came upon him lying outside a kiva entrance trussed up like a fowl.

"Aha, here you are lying, just as I thought," she said. "You must be hungry and cold, but you would have it that way and would not listen to me. Never mind, this may teach you something, and I have come to help you." She slipped a turkey feather beneath him and covered him with the other, and, just as before, they increased and he was at least soon warm. "Now you stay here until I come again."

Then she returned to her own house to think over the bad situation. "Why did that bad Hasohkata take my young friend," she thought bitterly, "and how can I get him back again? That man in the kiva is a bad one so he will not want to give up my grandson. I am going to call someone in here." So she went to the kiva entrance and raised her voice in a shrill, far-reaching summons, "All my people come to me here. Do not tarry—be quick about it."

Like magic, from all sides there came running on swift, padded feet all animals of prey. The bear, the wild cat, the panther—all such animals, and with them came Uncle Mole so that the kiva was entirely filled.

"What now? Why do you call us in such haste," they asked curiously.

"Yes, that Hasohkata has hung up my grandchild to smoke," she said, and indeed the youth was placed across the hatchway in exactly the same way that meat is hung for smoking. "So now I want you to help me get the lad away from this bad person."

In the meantime Hasohkata began to taunt the youth, "Now are you cold enough up there by this time?" or "Is it the way you like it up there now?" and so on, until at last Spider Woman and her people arrived at the kiva. Mole had scampered along ahead through an underground passage and sat awaiting them under the floor of the kiva. Hasohkata invited them to

[103]

come down and, looking in, Spider Woman could see the drawing of the game of chance on the floor by the fireplace. She had brought a cup game with her, so she called down.

"We have come to play a game with you. You are smoking my grandchild out here, and we have come to beat you at gaming and win him back."

"All right," he said laughing confidently, "maybe it will be as you say, maybe not. Come right in and we will see." So they entered and filled the entire kiva.

"Now who will commence?" asked Spider Woman.

"You will," said Hasohkata, "because you wanted it this way."

Spider Woman was glad of this and immediately set out her four gaming cups on the north of the fireplace. The mole, under the floor, reached up and put the ball under one of the cups, but he pushed it up hard so it would not fall out in case that cup should be chosen and thrown down by the player.

"Now guess which cup the ball is under, and we will see if you are right," said Spider Woman.

He thought about it a long time, then he threw down one of the cups. The ball was not under it. He threw down another one, but neither was the ball under that one.

"Now that is enough. You have not found it," said Spider Woman.

So she put down the cups again, and, just as before, the mole reached up slyly and fastened the ball securely in the top, and again Hasohkata was challenged which cup the ball was under. Again he threw down two cups without winning.

"My, who are you?" he said. "You must be somebody! Why are you trying to take all my things away from me? You have beaten me, so take your young man along."

Spider Woman then threw one of the cups, and the ball appeared and she said, "You can only play games with lads."

This made Hasohkata very angry, and he refused to let Chorzhvukiquole go. Now outside the kiva grew some very strong kwingwi, a bush having very strong branches. Hasohkata told them that if they could pull up a certain amount of this, either by breaking it off or uprooting it, he would then consider himself beaten. No sooner did Mole hear this proposal than he quickly crept underground and soon gnawed off the biggest roots and a great deal of the brush. The others did not know anything about this, so when Spider Woman said, "Now let us pull this out and see whether we can do it," they were very uneasy.

But at Spider Woman's command they all fell to tugging at it and in a short time had pulled up so much, even parts of the roots, that Hasohkata confessed himself beaten even before they had pulled up all Mole had loosened. "All right, you have beaten me," he said. "You take along all that I have and you will be rich."

So they returned to the kiva and untied the youth. "Now," said Hasohkata as they reentered the kiva, "take with you all of my things, because you have beaten me twice." The kiva was filled with bows, quivers, arrows, belts and many such things that he had won unfairly from those who had visited him and whom he had killed.

So they gathered the things together, but when they had done so Spider Woman asked, "But what shall we do to you who have killed so many of our fine young men?"

"You have taken all my things," he growled. "Now you go and let me alone."

"Oh no, you are dangerous," said Spider Woman. "That would leave you free to get more things and kill more people. We are going to destroy you for being so wicked."

Then all the animals who had come with Spider Woman fell on the man and destroyed him, and Spider Woman told the youth that he no longer would have to avoid going to the west because the dangerous one was no more. Then she thanked the animals and sent them back to their homes, while Chorzhvukiquole and she returned to her kiva.

The next day she led him to the place in the sky through which the eagles had carried him. Looking down through it they could see nothing —it looked just as it does when one looks up at the sky. Spider Woman placed sticks and grass around the opening to make it look like a spider hole and over it she spun a great web. Then she told Chorzhvukiquole to get on her back, and, still spinning, she made a fine silver thread that unwound until it placed them on the earth. She bade him shut his eyes lest the great height make him dizzy, and the next thing he knew they had landed in a familiar field not far from his mother's house. He thanked Spider Woman earnestly for all her goodness to him and made his way leaping to seek out his family. As he neared the village one of the neighbors saw him and called out to his parents.

"Someone has come. Your child has come."

But the parents could not believe their good fortune and returned sadly, "Alas, he will never come again. He is forever gone."

Then Chorzhvukiquole leapt in, shouting in glad boy-fashion, "Yes, I have come, I have come."

"Who are you?" said the unbelieving father.

"Why do you not know your own Chorzhvukiquole?"

"Nay, you are not that one—the eagles carried him away," said the father.

"Yes, but I am back," the lad insisted.

"Yes, you have come. Truly you have returned to us," said the father, convinced at last. His mother ran to him full of joy and gratitude. Then his sisters ran in to embrace him for they had grieved over him sorely, the more so because they had been so angry with him before he left. When a glowing pinyon fire had been made, they all sat about it to listen with bated breath to his thrilling adventures. And when Chorzhvukiquole told them he would now help them they were very happy. This is just the way it all happened.

The Children
and the Hummingbird

WHEN THE GODS withhold rain for one year it is bad, but when a drought lasts for four or five years hope grows weak and tired like corn plants without rain. That is how it was at Oraibi one time long ago.

The first year the ears of the corn had just begun to ripen when the frost came and killed them. The next year the drought delayed the growth so that the ears were just beginning to form when the frost destroyed the plants. By frost the next year the ears had not even formed, and the fourth year the drought had lasted so long that the plants were spindling and weak from the first. It was a terrible time! All the corn stored in previous bountiful years had at last been eaten, and there was nothing left. Thoroughly disheartened, many left the village to seek new homes, feeling that they could not be much worse off even though they did not better themselves much. The ones who remained planted their corn the fifth year, praying to Muiyinwuh to remember their need and cause the corn to thrive. But alas! the drought was worse if anything, and the corn grew tired and withered almost before it was out of the ground.

There was nothing to do now but leave their houses and see if they might not find food among some more fortunate people, and famine sped them on in desperation. In that terrible time of hunger and fear, two little children—a brother and sister—were left behind in that gaunt, deserted village. They knew not what to do—they knew no place to go, for encircling this poor place where they had always lived lay the vast Unknown. There was nothing to do, after their first mad panic of running as far into the wilderness as they dared, but to stay where they were and hope that they would be missed and someone would return for them. They thought surely that Masauwuh had snatched their parents and was driving the others so closely that the children had been forgotten.

The lad set himself bravely to the task of caring for his little sister, here and there gleaning some root or berry that kept them from absolute starvation and trying to cheer and comfort her. One day he thought he might make her forget how lonely and hungry she was, so he fashioned a little bird from the pith of a dry sunflower stalk.

"The great Spider Woman made all the birds of clay and made them come alive, so thus have I made one for you, and when you toss it into the air the breeze will make it look as if it too were alive," he said handing her the plaything. "Would that the tender Earth Mother might see us, or that we had her gift for making a tiny morsel of food increase."

The child was delighted with her plaything, and seeing that she was playing joyously he left to see if he could not find some root or forgotten seeds that would serve to stay their hunger. After playing with the bird in various ways, the girl began to pretend that it was a real, live one and tossed it high in the air to watch it flutter about before dropping back to her hand or falling to the earth. Imagine her surprise then when at last she threw it and it stayed in the air, skimming hither and thither, a real hummingbird, until at last it flew from her sight.

When the boy returned he found his little sister, whom he had left playing so gaily with her sunflower pith bird, now sitting quiet and sad. "Hao, little sister, where is the pretty bird I made you?"

"Yes, the bad little thing flew away and left me all alone," she complained.

At first he thought that she meant she had lost it in her play, and he could not believe her when she kept insisting that the bird had come to life and really flown away. It looked as if everything had determined to desert them, even the poor toy that had brought his sister a moment's happiness. In addition, he was very sad because he had been unable to find a scrap of anything they could eat, and he knew no new place to search.

The next morning, as the two sat together while the lad tried to comfort and amuse his sister the best he could, the tiny bird returned and darted into one of the crannies in the stone walls of their house.

"My birdie has come back," screamed out the girl excitedly. "See, my bird has flown in there."

"Where?" asked the boy, who had seen nothing.

"Why it flew past us and went in that hole there in the wall. Get it for me brother. It was such a good little playmate. I love it."

Very doubtingly, the lad thrust his hand into the opening and was surprised to find that it was quite large enough, but though he felt in every corner the bird was not there. There was something else there though, and he drew it into the light with eagerness, for it felt under his fingers like an ear of corn—maybe a forgotten ear of dry corn. He could hardly believe his eyes when he drew it forth to find it was corn and not a dry ear but green and fresh.

"Thanks, thanks," they shouted gratefully, while their great eyes burned at the sight of real food. Then they roasted it, and when it was divided ate of it ravenously to the smallest kernel and then sucked the cob. Hardly had they finished when, from the opening the boy had so carefully searched, there was a flash of color and the bird skimmed past them. Even the boy saw it this time.

"It is Totca, the hummingbird," gasped the boy.

"It is my friend, my friend," called the little girl.

The next day as they sat on the doorstep the little bird flew past them and again disappeared within the same hole. When the boy thrust in his hand he drew forth another ear, and it was a larger one. They were so happy about it that they could talk of nothing else but the wonder of it and every little while would run to see if the bird had returned. The next day and the next the bird returned, each time leaving an ear larger than the one before, so that the children became quite well fed. But on the fifth day, though it came back, when the lad put his hand in the hole, there was no corn there, and he brought out only the tiny bird figure he had made from the sunflower pith.

He was very sad about this, for the little bird seemed to be all that stood between them and starvation. Quite desperately he took the small thing in his hands and said, "You are something living. You go and hunt for our parents. They have left us but perhaps you can find them. Please bring us something more to eat. Go south and look for our father and mother. My sister is small and grieves for my mother's arms."

But to his imploring eyes there appeared no sign of life in the inert pith figure, and so he turned to his sister and asked her in what way she had made the bird fly. Confidently, she took the small figure by the wings and, lifting a smiling, trustful face to him, said, "This is the way I did it." And when she had tossed it in the air the hummingbird again came alive and flew away.

After the bird had left the children staring at it in open-mouthed wonder, it flew until it came to a great rock upon which it lit to rest and look about it. Turning to the south, it spied afar a cactus plant on which flamed a single brilliant red blossom. At once it flew thither and hunted about until it found an opening beneath the plant into which it flew. Beyond this opening it found a roomy kiva where grass and some herbs were growing. At the north end of the kiva was another opening through which it passed to find itself in another kiva. Here it found some corn with pollen on it and ate of it. Passing through an opening in this kiva, it found itself in a third, where there was an abundance of grass, herbs and corn of all kinds. Here lived Muiyinwuh, the god of all growing things. All kinds of birds flew about in this kiva, but it was the sharp eyes of the hummingbirds that saw the newcomer first.

"Somebody strange has come in," they chirruped to Muiyinwuh.

"Who has come in?" asked the god. "Let him come before me."

Fearlessly the little bird flew over and lit on the great arm of Muiyinwuh — there it waited.

"Why have you come here?" the god inquired.

"Yes," said the bird boldly, "what are you doing down here? Why have you allowed bad people to influence you to stay here in your kiva and not think of how the people up there on earth are doing? Why have you listened to them? Your fields up there are dry and barren. The corn all grew tired and died. It has not rained there and nothing grows. There at Oraibi the people all left, and there are only two small children there alone. Even they would have starved had not Spider Woman made me live so that I might bring food to them. You had better come up there and look after things."

At the bold words of the tiny creature there was absolute silence, but it could be seen that Muiyinwuh was thinking long thoughts. "All right," he said at last, "I am thinking about the matter."

"I wish you would give me something for those children who must be very hungry for they have had nothing at all today."

"Certainly, you must take all you want for yourself and the children," consented the god.

So the bird broke off the nicest, juiciest roasting ear he could find, and it became small so he could carry it. Flying back, he put it in the same hole where it became large again. When the children saw the bird return they were filled with hope, but the lad was almost afraid to put in his hand, for they were very hungry again and he dreaded the disappointment if there were nothing there. But the girl was sure her little friend had brought them something and insisted that he get it. They were wild with joy when the boy drew forth the finest, juiciest ear they had ever seen.

"Oh, thank you, Totca, that you have pitied us. Thank you that you have brought us something to eat. It is because of you that we are alive. Through you our hunger is satisfied. We are very happy about it, but we pray you not to leave us for you are all we have."

"Yes, I have pitied you," said the bird kindly. "For that reason I have come again. I shall live here close by you until all is well with you again."

"And will you please try to find our father and mother?" asked the lad.

"I will look for them," answered the bird and flew away.

Instead of going to the south as the boy had suggested, the bird flew over the fields to the west of Oraibi and then went north. Its sharp eyes searched every part of the mesa land until finally, at a place called Toho, it found the parents. They were pitiably thin and weak because they were living on nothing but cactus.

They did not see the hummingbird, but when it flew past them the father said, "Something is passing here." The bird flew past them again and when they saw it the man asked, "Who are you flying about here where there have been no living things but my wife and me?" The bird did not answer but poised in the air with its wings moving and listened to what the man had to say.

"In your flying here and there have you seen any food, little bird? If you know of any, have pity on us and show us where it is." For there were no living creatures about that part of the country, and the man thought the bird must have some place to get food. They were, therefore, disappointed when the hummingbird, after listening to them, flew away without making any answer.

Hummingbird flew right back to the children,

and the boy ran to meet it with the question, "Did you find our parents?"

"Yes, I found them," answered the bird.

"Both of them?" asked the children anxiously.

"Yes, both, but alas they have very little to eat. They are hungry and they are very thin."

"Oh, little bird, do be quick and take them that which you were going to give us," implored the children.

In the meantime Muiyinwuh, after thinking over what Hummingbird had told him, decided to go to the earth and see how things were going there and whether the things the bird had told him were true. He ascended to the next kiva to stay there four days, and during that time it rained at Oraibi. Then he went to the next kiva, and during his four days' stay there it rained at Oraibi again. When he ascended to the next kiva it rained considerably in the deserted village, so that when he came out on the earth he found grasses and herbs growing nicely. The little bird and its friends had been busily sowing corn in the fields so that it, too, began to put forth lusty green blades.

From a distance the two parents at Toho could see the clouds that looked to be hovering over Oraibi, and they decided to return there and see. They did not know their children were there and had been there all the time. In fact they did not know how they had been separated from them in that mad flight to escape the famine, for all had been too crazed with hunger to think clearly. When they stumbled into the village, weak and weary, they could hardly believe their eyes when their two children leapt upon them and gave them from their ear of corn and some water.

Others who had fled the village also saw the precious rain clouds over their deserted Oraibi and returned to their homes. Soon the village came to life — full of people. The corn the birds had planted thrived and bore abundantly and Muiyinwuh blessed them. When the little boy and girl grew up they and their descendents became the village chiefs and owners of Oraibi, and they never forgot the little Totca who had saved them in their great need.

The Antelope Maid

MANY GRANDFATHERS BACK, in a village of the Zuni, two sons of the village chief were running a race with each other. There was a place not far from the village called Aamusha, where it was known that one should not go. It was well known that someone very dangerous lived at this place, for many young men had disappeared after venturing near there. These two lads knew about this, but they raced along the path just the same. Indeed, they scoffed at the idea that anything could catch them, fleet of foot as they were, and it was exciting to go to a place that had been forbidden. So they ran along joyously until they came to a high bluff, and when they were close upon it they heard a voice calling to them.

"Come here. There is something very beautiful here," it called coaxingly.

The lads were so startled that they stopped short and looked all about them. "Oh, no, there is nothing there," they replied, knowing that they should approach no closer.

"Yes, you come and see for yourselves. There is something very beautiful here," the voice insisted.

And, though the boys knew full well the reputed danger of the place, they could not resist drawing just a bit closer in order to see what might be seen. When they had come quite near, there suddenly appeared on the top of the bluff a most beautiful maiden. Her rounded figure was draped in a wonderfully bordered white blanket, and her hair was so luxuriant that it formed two great whorls above her ears. When they saw that her head was crowned with horns they knew that she must be Antelope Maid. Surely one so beautiful could not be dangerous. As they stared at her with open-mouthed admiration, the maiden suddenly bent forward and drew in her breath in a deep, long gust. In an instant the elder lad rose swiftly from the ground and was sucked upward until he stood beside the mana. Then she looked down on the younger lad and, smiling derisively, taunted him.

"You see how it is. I have your brother and even though you offer me many beads, the thing you Zuni value most, I shall not give you back your brother for I do not want your beads. I have enough beads."

Startled and repentant for their disobedience, the younger brother ran swiftly back to the village and sought out his father.

"Why do you look so wild and why do you come alone? Where is your brother?" the father asked.

"Yes, we were racing there by that dangerous place called Aamusha when a most beautiful mana called us to come nearer, and no sooner had we done so than in an eye's wink she had with her breath sucked my brother up beside her."

"Alas, why must it always be that way that youth cannot be warned but must see for itself," cried out the father. "Yes, someone dangerous has always lived there, and we have never been able to do anything about it. You run and find the Twins and ask them to give us help in this matter." First, however, he cut a round piece from the middle of a buckskin and made a ball which he tied to a stick; next he fashioned an arrow which he fletched with bluebird and parrot feathers, and giving the boy some tobacco to carry with these offerings he sped him on his way.

With swift feet the youth ran southward until he was stopped by the sound of voices calling back and forth. Two small figures appeared in the distance, romping about and playing together. He recognized them at once as those two Little but Mighty Ones, the Twins. Instead of going to them, however, he continued to the house of their grandmother, Spider Woman, who, when he had explained his mission, went out and called loudly to them.

"Stop your playing and come here. Someone has come." But they played on without paying the slightest attention to her.

So she called again and this time more commandingly, "Stop your foolishness and come here. Someone has come to see you."

So, romping and tumbling over each other, they returned and received with great pleasure the presents the boy's father had made for them. "These have I brought you. Way over there at Aamusha lives a very pretty mana who drew up my brother with a deep breath, and now my father has sent you these things and wants to know what you think about it and what you can do for us. She says she will not give him back for beads."

The Twins listened carefully and then said, "You go westward until you come upon our Uncle Mole. You will come to a hollow place where the ladder ends are sticking out — he lives there. Ask him what he thinks about it."

So the lad ran quickly to the westward until he came to the kiva of Uncle Mole. When he had explained the matter, Mole thought seriously about it for a while and then said, "You go northward to my Uncle Storm and see what he has to say about such a matter."

So the lad stretched out his legs and ran to the north, and at last came to an opening through which a strong breeze was blowing.

"This must be the place," he decided, and with his thought a strong wind issued from the opening.

"Come down," invited a gusty voice. Proceeding to do so, he came upon a Hopi man whom he recognized as Storm, Hukangwaa. There was a handsome man! He was nicely dressed, wearing two buckskins tied crossways over his broad chest and a bandoleer swung over his mighty shoulders. He had a huruhka on his head and a bordered kilt about his loins. His body was painted warrior-fashion, and there were black lines across his cheeks.

"I see you have come," said Hukangwaa.

"Yes, way over there near where we live a pretty mana drew my brother up beside her on the cliff—with her breath she did it. She had horns on her head and she is very dangerous they say. My father thought the Twins might help us, but they sent me to Uncle Mole and now he has sent me to you."

"Well, that is all right," said Hukangwaa, "but we had better smoke and then we can tell better what we think about it."

So he got out a pipe to test what sort of a lad this one was and the youth smoked, swallowing all the smoke. It took especial courage to do this, and when he had finished he turned proudly to his host and said, "Itaha, my uncle."

"Yes, you have done that very right, Itiaya, my nephew," Storm replied much pleased. "You are surely my nephew. Now what is it you want? What has happened over there?"

The lad repeated his story earnestly. "My older brother and I were racing there at Aamusha when a beautiful maiden called to us. When we came nearer, with a deep strong breath she drew my brother up beside her. She wore horns and is that Antelope Mana, I think. Our beads she does not want, and my father sent me out to see if I could get some mighty one to help me.

[122]

The Twins sent me to Uncle Mole and he sent me on to you. So what about it now?"

Uncle Storm began to think about all this very deeply; at last he nodded his head and said, "You go to Walpi and see the Snake People there. They used to have their dances here at Tokonabi and were driven away because the snakes bit somebody. Go to them. They should have something to say about this."

Now Walpi was a great way off, but the lad hastened thither as fast as his legs could go and at last found the mesa home of the Snake People. Handsome folk, they were dressed like warriors and like Snake People.

"Why are you here?" they asked as the strange lad entered their kiva.

"Yes, we were racing over there, my brother and I, and when we came to Aamusha someone called sweetly to us and said, 'You come here, come up here. There is something beautiful here.' Then she drew him up beside her with a deep strong breath. The Twins sent me to Uncle Mole when I sought their aid. Uncle Mole sent me to Uncle Storm. And Uncle Storm sent me to you. Now are you the ones and what now? Have you any thoughts about it?"

"We shall see," they said offering him a pipe. Again the stripling swallowed all the smoke, and it could be seen that the Snake People were much impressed by his hardiness. "You are truly our nephew," they declared. "Tell us now what you want."

The lad was quite tired of repeating his story by this time, but he began again very patiently.

[123]

"Yes, we were racing there and the dangerous maiden drew my brother up beside her with her breath. She said she would not give him back even if we brought her stone beads because she does not want our beads."

The Snake People began to think very long thoughts about this, looking into the smoke of their pipes and nodding their heads wisely. "Yes, she does not want your beads," they said at last. "You see this?" and held up a prayer stick. "The maiden wants paho; she does not want your beads. Yes, she wants such a paho. You look at this paho well and then make one like it. No, we had better make one for you, for it is very important that it be made just right. You take this along and look at it closely, then make many more like it and give them to the maiden. These she wants." He took the paho with many thanks and started eagerly back on his long homeward journey.

When he reached home he told them all he had done and all the great ones he had met. He next showed them how to make the paho, and, after they had made a great number of them, they set forth for the place where the mana had sucked up the young man. With them were Spider Woman, Uncle Mole, the Twins and Uncle Storm, who had come to lend their help. Spider Woman could not be seen though, for she followed her usual custom of changing into a tiny spider and riding upon the right ear of Puukonhoya.

Arriving at the bluff the old father of the boys

[124]

called out, "We have come to get that boy you drew up there."

"Well, what have you brought with you?" said the horned mana as she appeared suddenly at the top of the bluff. "I will not have any of your old stone beads."

"Yes, we know about that," replied the father. "We have brought paho that are very something."

He had no sooner finished speaking than Uncle Storm lifted up the whole party to the top of the bluff. Like a flash the maiden turned and fled before them toward her house. But Storm pushed them all close upon her flying heels and into the house behind her. "Show me what you have brought then," the mana demanded, facing them with furiously flashing eyes.

"This we have brought, this here," the father cried, waving a paho before her enraged face.

"Thanks," she said, her expression changing as if by magic to one of pleasure. "Yes, these are what I want. Of course, I will give you the lad but we must first play a game." She spread some sand on the floor and said, "Now, you play first."

Then the Hopi planted different kinds of seed in the sand, and when they had planted the paho around in the sand to form a border, the seeds sprouted into plants.

"Thanks, thanks, you certainly know something. I had heard about this. These I want and I will certainly let you have the youth. But we must make a race first. We will follow the Sun."

So she and the younger brother arranged for a race. The lad mounted an eagle breath feather, but the mana turned herself into a swift snake called Tokchii. Off they started side by side, but it was not long before it was seen that the maiden was gaining rapidly. Round the Sun they circled, speeding like light, then back they turned with the maiden far in the lead. But now Spider Woman took a part. Hastily plucking a reed growing beside her, she put it to her lips and, pointing it at the young man, drew in a mighty breath. Instantly the youth shot forward. Another deep breath, and with lightning speed he shot ahead of the maiden and arrived at the goal far ahead of her.

"All right, take the young man along then. You have beaten me," said the Antelope Maid. Going quickly to an inner chamber she dragged forth the elder brother, half-dead.

In that room were the bones of many young men who had perished there. It was because the people had ceased to offer paho to her that the Antelope Maid had seized the young men and slain them. Now that the younger brother had found out what she wanted and she had again received paho, the maiden was reconciled. The people promised that they would never again neglect to offer to her proper paho. Aamusha no longer harbors someone dangerous, and from that time on no more young men were captured and destroyed.

The Giant Elk

OF ALL THE FEARFUL CREATURES that roamed the world and harassed the Peaceful People there was none more formidable than the Giant Elk. His magnificent antlers were like cruel giant hands with upturned palms and bony fingers, and their spread was many feet wide. The Twins, Puukonhoya and Palunhoya, had long wished to rid the world of this monster, so at last they started out one day in quest of him. Meeting Uncle Mole, they asked him if he could tell them of the monster's whereabouts.

"Indeed! That I can," said Mole. "He has spent the morning neck deep in a nearby pool into which he waded to escape the flies and feed on some tender water plants there. He has but just left it to lie down in the green valley beside it."

"That is good. We thank you for making it easy for us to find him," exulted Puukonhoya, the elder and bolder of the Twins. "We will set right off to kill this creature that has so long tormented us."

"But slowly, slowly, little nephews," warned Mole in alarm. "He is not to be attacked openly but with skill and cunning. He is most mighty and will surely kill you if you approach him boldly. When he is aroused he strikes killing blows with those great forefeet of his and gores deeply with his vicious, many-pronged antlers. Besides this, there is none so difficult to hunt as he. His sharp scent and quick ears make it impossible to approach him unobserved, and he can run like the wind."

"Yes, we are going no matter what the difficulty or the danger," the rash Twins insisted with one accord, "for we have vowed to rid the earth of this dangerous one, and we could not show our faces for shame if we were afraid to encounter him."

"Nay, then, if you are determined to keep to this perilous undertaking, at least allow me to help you or else your mighty grandmother, Spider Woman, would not easily forgive me. I can approach him in my underground runs and prepare a way for you to retreat in case he presses on you too closely."

With the utmost reluctance the intrepid youths consented, and straightway the pink snout of Uncle Mole had begun to burrow into the earth and his out-turned paws to shovel so furiously that he seemed to push himself forward into the earth as a powerful swimmer does in the water. In an incredibly short time he had hollowed out a chamber, and here he bade the Twins await him. Returning to his digging, he made a second chamber below this and below this another, and another, until he had made four chambers in all. Then he dug a long tunnel that stopped right under the huge dozing body of the Giant Elk lying in the green valley close by Mt. Taylor.

Then, very gently, Uncle Mole plucked a bit of soft hair from a spot directly over the great, throbbing heart of the Giant Elk. Then a bit more and a bit more, but adroit and gentle though he was he was unable to escape the vigilance of the monster, who suddenly bent his great head and glared down on this tiny disturber of his rest.

"Be not wroth, Greatest One, you surely would not begrudge me a bit of your wonderfully soft hair to make a bed for my children."

Mole's words and humility so flattered Giant Elk that he allowed him to continue plucking, and soon there was enough fur removed to leave a large spot over the animal's heart quite bare. This accomplished, he returned swiftly to the Twins to tell them that now all was in readiness for them to proceed.

The Twins then began a stealthy approach toward their prey, careful that the wind was blowing away from him. As soon as they were within throwing distance, they hurled the magic lightning given them by Tawa. Wounded and enraged, the huge creature leapt to his feet—a terrible sight to behold. His widely distended nostrils snorted forth rage as he sprang to his long legs and he charged upon his tiny foes. Undaunted, they continued to hurl their lightning, but when he was right upon them and had reared to strike them down and trample them with his vicious forefeet they retreated to the upper chamber wise little Mole had dug for them. When the infuriated Elk tried to gore them with his antlers, they would not reach so deep.

Then he charged more furiously, thrusting his great horns downward murderously, but the Twins had fled to the second chamber. The breath of Giant Elk came so heavily because of his great exertions that it sounded like the storm wind soughing above them, but he exerted his mighty strength and charged again so terrifically that his horns plowed way down into the second chamber, and the Twins had barely escaped into the one below. Should the colossal strength of the monster enable him to reach the third chamber, they had but one more place of retreat. The sides of Giant Elk were now heaving like storm-wracked ocean billows, and his breath came in cruel, shuddering gasps, whose gusts sent the Twins speeding to the fourth chamber. They saw above them the bare place that Uncle Mole had plucked above his heart and desperately threw their lightning directly upon it. One more mighty effort the Great One made, but it was too much for him, wounded in the heart as he had been, so at last, with a force that made the earth tremble, the Giant Elk fell dead.

When no further sound of onslaught reached the fourth chamber, the Twins crept forth with great caution and found there the great slain body of their foe. Here they were faced with a new difficulty. In that land of little game the meat must be saved for flesh, and game was too precious for even a little to be wasted. Here was a great hillock of meat, and they had no knife with which to cut it up. While they were trying to think what to do, a tiny voice squeaked out nearby them and, turning, they beheld the Chipmunk, Kohone.

"Little but Mighty Ones, I wish to be the first to thank you for putting an end to this dangerous one. Spider Woman is very proud of you and has sent me to cut up his body for you."

It seemed impossible that this tiny creature could accomplish anything on this great carcass; but soon the sharp teeth of Kohone started, and before long the mountain of flesh was neatly divided.

The Twins were greatly pleased with the little creature's fine work. "That was well done," said Puukonhoya. "We thank you, little brother. You have served us greatly, for we were very weary after our fight with the Giant Elk and, furthermore, had no way of cutting up his body. This you did with your sharp teeth, and from this time forward you shall wear a symbol of your service to us." Bending down, he dipped two fingers in the blood of the Giant Elk, then drew them gently along the sleek, velvet back of Kohone. Two dark stripes appeared, and these marks of honor Kohone and his children wear to the present day. What the gods do stands forever!

The Coyote and the Water Serpent

IN A TIME VERY VERY WHEN, the Coyote and the
Water Serpent were great friends. They lived not
far from each other and so were able to visit back
and forth in each other's kivas. They were both
young, but the Water Serpent grew so rapidly
that soon he got to be very, very long; in fact,
even though he would coil himself up in the
smallest possible form, it came about that he
would fill almost the entire kiva and leave only a
small space near the fireplace for Coyote to sit, all
crouched up and uncomfortable. The Water
Serpent grew to be very proud of his great size
and could not help calling attention to it and
boasting of it continually, much to the Coyote's
disgust and envy.

"Am I not of a remarkable size?" he would
say to Coyote, rearing up his head so as to gloat
over his smooth coils. "And I am going to be
much larger when I am fully grown. You had
better enlarge your kiva or soon there will be no
room for you at all." And the entire time of their
visits he would talk of his size until it was time to
go when he would uncoil slowly, saying, "Now

I have visited you. It is your turn to come and see me."

After a time this constant boasting began to wear on Coyote and rankle in his heart. It did not set at all well to have his friend so much the larger. Truly it was an impressive sight to see the Water Serpent quite fill up a whole kiva and most humiliating to have to sit all scrunched up in the tiny space that was left. Soon Coyote's mind became entirely occupied with the desire to increase his size so as to fill the Water Serpent's kiva when he should return the visit. It really became unendurable, so he burst out to his friend one day, "Well, you know that I, too, am going to be of much greater size. My tail will grow to be very long someday, and it is much more difficult to grow a long tail with fur on it than the smooth kind. In fact, I am likely to be much larger than you once I get started."

"Yes, it may happen to come about that way," leered Water Serpent. "Me, though, I have never seen such a coyote." And then it took the great reptile so long to uncoil itself that when the head had been out some time the long body was still unfolding itself within the kiva, and Coyote's heart was bitter with envy.

When the last tip of the tail had disappeared, Coyote broke out disgustedly, "My, but that Water Serpent is disagreeable and swollen up with pride. He is so proud he might be the Great Plumed Serpent himself. Yaaa, I suppose he does think so. Such pride about nothing more than a tail and one at that that starts right

[133]

behind his ears! Not a really proper tail. No body, no legs—a tail, no more. If one had such a tail, besides a body, then he would be very something. I must do something about this matter."

So he thought and thought. First he tried to make his tail grow by magic. He rubbed it with this and that and sang songs over it, but the tail remained the same. He did not have the right nahu. So he became very angry and shouted, "Bah, Spider Woman, herself, could not make that tail grow, but I will show that I can manage something anyway. Now, let me think."

He scratched his head with his left front paw, then he scratched his head with his right front paw. Finally, he doubled back both his hind legs and scratched his head with them. Looking thoughtfully between them, he noticed that his tail was lying on top of a piece of cedar bough, and this gave him a wonderful idea.

"Hao, now let me go and hunt something." So he ran quickly to a place where a great deal of cedar grew. He was very excited and happy and pulled off a great quantity of the bark and carried it home. Then he thought very deeply, saying to himself, "How shall I contrive a tail that will deceive the sharp eyes of the Water Serpent?" Finally he began to work the bark to make it pliable; next he laid it out into the semblance of a fine long tail on the kiva floor; then he wrapped it carefully with yucca leaves to make it strong. Still, it did not look like much of a tail. It would never deceive the Water Serpent.

"I have it—I must cover it with hair," he said at last.

So he pulled out a lot of hair from his own body and cleverly gummed it over the tail until it looked very natural. When he had tied it securely to his own short one, he chuckled with joy at his cleverness. "Spider Woman, herself, could not have done better," he boasted. A most dangerous thing to say, you will agree.

He could hardly wait to finish his breakfast the next morning, so anxious was he to return the visit of the Water Serpent. He was very eager to witness his friend's astonishment. The kiva of the Water Serpent was quite roomy, so he had a fine time circling around it, dragging his fine long tail behind him before sitting down to talk to his friend. The Water Serpent watched him, smiling disturbingly at the new bushy tail, but to the disappointment of the Coyote he made no remarks. But, to himself, the Serpent said, "Now truly this is a strange thing. The tail did not used to be like that. I wonder how this can be."

They talked and talked, each about his own size, and had a lovely, long visit, until Coyote said he must be going home to dinner. He had another fine time uncoiling his tail before the interested eyes of the Water Serpent and said condescendingly to his friend as he started up the ladder, "Now, whenever you feel that way, you must come over and see me again too. It is your turn now."

The Serpent politely promised to do so, and the Coyote walked slowly away so as to drag the tail as long as possible. "Yaaa," he chuckled to himself, "Water Serpent may be long, but he is not so clever as I, and he did not find out how it is with my tail. He is just a tail and no more," and he smiled happily as he untied the false tail from his own, which was quite weary from the extra weight.

True to his word and not long after, the Serpent came to return the visit. The crafty Coyote, who had been afraid lest the Serpent catch him unawares, was on the lookout, so he had no sooner caught a glimpse of his visitor approaching than he made haste to attach his artificial tail. When the Serpent entered, he was sitting by the fireplace and affected the greatest surprise at the sight of his visitor. "What a surprise that you should come. My, but I am glad to see you. I did not know that you would feel this way—come right in," he said pleasantly.

The Water Serpent tried to enter, but he had grown considerably since his last visit, and the Coyote's new tail took up so much room that he found he could not get himself all in. "You see how it is," said the Serpent, pleased with this proof of his increasing size. "I have been growing so much since my last visit that I cannot get in anymore."

"Oh no, that is not it," contradicted the Coyote. "It is because I have grown so much that there is not room for you. Let me go out and you will see."

So Coyote circled about so as to make the

most of his tail and, coiling it around, took a seat at the top of the kiva's entrance where he could still hold conversation with his friend. They talked about the same thing they always did, but by and by the Coyote grew cold and began to wish that his huge friend would go home. Water Serpent had no such thought, for he was very comfortable down in the kiva by the warm fire. The colder Coyote grew, the hotter grew his wrath, and he spent his time thinking how he would make the Water Serpent sit outside in the cold as he was now doing. When a long time had passed, the Serpent said lazily, "Well, I guess I had better be going home to my dinner," and the Coyote was so cold and so angry that he did not even wait for his guest to get entirely out before rushing down to warm himself.

Nor could he refrain from saying, "Look out for me when I come to return your visit, for I shall be much larger then."

"Yes, maybe it will be that way," said the Serpent with a smile that angered the Coyote still further.

"Oh, such pride," he growled crossly. "I will most certainly have to pay him back for keeping me out in the cold like this." All the time he was eating his dinner he was thinking a great deal, and so, as soon as he had gulped it down, he started off to the cedar grove again. Bringing back a huge armful of bark and yucca leaves, he made a long addition to his tail and made it much finer and thicker. He would have liked to return the visit immediately but decided to wait for a very cold day. When such a day came, he set off in hot haste to the Serpent's kiva.

Arriving there, he called out, "Hao, is the friend at home?"

"Yes. I am here by the fire. Come in."

Such a grand sight the Coyote was as he entered the kiva and strutted proudly about, round and round, until the kiva was crowded to its very walls.

"Well," said the Serpent in surprise, "Truly, it is as you said. I had better get out and talk to you from up there." So, leaving the kiva, the Water Serpent coiled himself up in such a manner that it left his head close to the hatchway and enabled him to talk with his guest below.

It was extremely cold, and the Coyote smiled happily in the thought that, while he was warm and comfortable, the Serpent was in exactly the same position in which he had so lately been. "Now you can freeze out there too. Now you can see how it is to be proud of nothing more than a great tail—one that has not even fur upon it."

The Water Serpent grew colder and colder and heartily wished that Coyote would take himself off, but Coyote had made up his mind to give the Serpent a good dose. It was only hunger that finally made him take his leave, and he paraded his tail with the usual slowness. Before the tail was nearly all out the Serpent slid back in, and he was for the first time angry with the Coyote.

"I am going to get even with you. I am going to pay you back. Get out of here, mischief-maker. You are always taking people's things. You are continually doing something bad. Last time I visited you you were not even polite enough to wait for me to get out of your kiva but rushed in and crowded my beautiful tail into the hot ashes and blistered it. I no longer want you for my friend, so get away from here and stay away." Then the Serpent crossly shoved the Coyote's slowly disappearing tail into the fire.

Of course, the tail of cedar and pinyon gum quickly caught fire, but Coyote did not know it because the tail was so long that he was far outside. He made his way homeward, turning now and then to admire the tail sweeping far behind. It was not until he had gone some little way that he noticed some smoke and flames behind him, but as there was no feeling in the false tail he thought it was simply some fire in the grass.

"Aha, the Hopi have set the grass afire," he said. "They must be trying to smoke me out. Maybe they will kill me. I am not going home now. I had better run away somewhere else."

He ran far to the westward because, whenever he looked behind, the fire followed him, and he thought he was being pursued. When he had reached the timber and, turning hopefully, saw that even that blazed behind him, he decided the only thing for him to do to escape his pursuers would be to run to the Little Colorado River and jump in. At no time did poor foolish Coyote suspect that it was the great false tail dragging behind him that was causing the fire.

At last the river bank was reached, but he paused on the bank for the waters were very angry. Then came the voice of the fire—hot and hungry. He plunged in frantically and tried to swim across but soon began to drift with the current. For miles he had been dragging behind him the unaccustomed weight of the long, long tail, and now he was overcome by weariness. So he was pulled beneath the swift waters to start on that journey to the Underworld that would henceforth be his home. Too bad that foolish Coyote should have boasted himself against Spider Woman—too bad he was so proud.

Further Reading

Fewkes, J. Walter. *Hopi Katcinas Drawn by Native Artists.* U.S. Bureau of American Ethnology, 21st Annual Report, 1899–1900. Washington, D.C.: Smithsonian Institution, 1903.

_____. "Sky-God Personations in Hopi Worship." *Journal of American Folklore* 15:14–32. 1902.

_____. Assisted by A.M. Stephen and J. G. Owens. *The Snake Ceremonials at Walpi.* In *A Journal of American Ethnology and Archaeology,* vol. 4. Boston and New York: Houghton Mifflin & Co., 1894.

_____. "A Suggestion As To The Meaning of Moki Snake Dance." In *Journal of American Folklore* 4:129–38. 1891.

Hough, Walter. *The Hopi Indians.* Cedar Rapids, Iowa: The Torch Press, 1915.

Mindeleff, Victor. *A Study of Pueblo Architecture, Tusayan and Cibola.* U.S. Bureau of American Ethnology, 8th Annual Report, 1886–87. Washington, D.C.: Smithsonian Institution, 1891, pp. 16–41.

Stephen, Alexander MacGregor. *Hopi Indians of Arizona.* Leaflet No. 14. Los Angeles: Southwest Museum, 1940. (Written ca. 1883–1893.)

_____. *Hopi Journal of Alexander M. Stephen.* 2 vols. New York: Columbia University Press, 1936. Reprinted by AMS Press, Inc., New York, 1969.

_____. "Hopi Tales." *Journal of American Folklore,* vol. 42, no. 63, Jan.–Mar. 1929, pp. 1–72, 187–91.

Stephen, Alexander MacGregor. "Legend of the Snake Order of the Moquis, as Told by Outsiders." *Journal of American Folklore*, vol. 1, no. 2, July–Sept. 1888, pp. 109–14.

Voth, H.R. "The Traditions of the Hopi." In *Field Columbian Museum Anthropological Series*, vol. 8, publication 96. Chicago: Field Columbian Museum, 1905.